THE WAFFLER

THE WAFFLER

Gail Donovan

Dial Books for Young Readers

an imprint of Penguin Group (USA) Inc.

Dial Books for Young Readers
A division of Penguin Young Readers Group
Published by the Penguin Group
Penguin Group(USA) Inc., 375 Hudson Street, New York, New York 10014, USA

USA / Canada / UK / Ireland / Australia / New Zealand / India / South Africa / China
Penguin Books Ltd, Registered Offices, 80 Strand, London WC2R 0RL, England
For more information about the Penguin Group visit penguin.com

Library of Congress Cataloging-in-Publication Data

Donovan, Gail, date.
The waffler / by Gail Donovan.   p. cm.
Summary: Fourth grader Monty can't ever make up his mind, but when a
school project tests his abilities, Monty has to decide—should he
follow what his teachers say, or do what he knows is right?
ISBN 978-0-8037-3920-8 (hardcover)
I. Title.
PZ7.D7227Waf 2013   [Fic]—dc23   2012031856

Printed in USA
1 3 5 7 9 10 8 6 4 2

Designed by Mina Chung

For my
twin

CONTENTS

FURRY FRIENDS

Monty wandered up and down the aisles, trying to make up his mind before somebody got mad that he was taking too long.

Too late. Here came his dad.

"What do you think?" asked his dad. "Did you decide?"

"I'm trying," said Monty.

"You know Sierra's got a game, right?"

"I know," said Monty.

"If you want me to drop you at home before the game, we need to leave soon. So make up your mind. Seriously."

"I *am*," objected Monty. "That's what I'm *doing*."

Monty's dad flipped open his cell phone. "Five

minutes," he warned, and walked away, tapping out a message on the phone.

The trouble with Monty was that he was a mind-changer. That didn't mean he changed other people's minds. It meant he changed his own. Constantly, according to his dad. And his mom. Also his step-dad. And stepmom. They all said he should stop changing his mind so much. He should be a mind-maker-upper.

Right now, what he had to make up his mind about was finding the right pet. He set out around the Pet Emporium one more time. A dog would be the best. If he could get a puppy he'd pick a Lab with chocolate-brown hair, just like him. But his dad had already said no dog, no way no how, and Monty knew that was final.

A fish? Monty wandered past the fish tanks. The whole fish area smelled like the time his mom had left the water in the wading pool too long and it got all green. Plus fish were boring. The birds were crazy loud. They made his head hurt.

Sierra came skipping up in her soccer uniform, high red socks and red shorts and a red shirt with the name of their dad's business on the back: *Pronto Painting*. Their dad's business slogan was *Do It Pronto*, which pretty much described their dad. He was in favor of making up your mind and getting things done *pronto*.

Their dad sponsored the team and helped coach, too, which Monty thought should maybe be against the rules because his dad just about had a heart attack every game. Their dad was crazy about soccer, and so was Sierra. This summer she'd been to some fancy sleepaway soccer camp. Monty wasn't crazy about soccer and he hadn't gone to any fancy camp. Instead, he'd gotten a guarantee that he could get a pet *if* he got off to a good start in fourth grade. Somehow Monty had made it through September without his teacher calling home for a "chat on what strategies will work for Monty," like last year's teacher. So now here he was: the first Saturday in October, searching the Pet Emporium for the perfect pet.

"Dad says if we leave soon we can stop for doughnuts," said Sierra.

"Cool," said Monty.

"So, what are you going to get?" she asked.

Looking at Sierra was kind of like looking in the mirror. They both had chocolate-brown hair, and hers was as short as his. They both had a few freckles splattered across the bridge of their noses. And they both had blue eyes.

"I don't know," said Monty, heading down the reptiles aisle. "Don't bug me."

"I'm not bugging!" said Sierra, tagging along. "I'm just asking! How about a snake?"

"I'm not stupid," said Monty. "Mom'll never say yes to a snake."

"She'll never say yes to anything," Sierra pointed out.

Monty's mom always said that Monty and Sierra and Aisha, who was their mom's new baby with their stepdad, were plenty of creatures in the house. She and Monty's dad had agreed that the pet would stay at his dad's house. If Monty hadn't gone along—no pet. But Monty was hoping he could change his mom's mind, so he could bring his pet to her house, too. That meant not picking a snake.

"Tarantula?" suggested Sierra.

"No way!" said Monty. Ditto the snake problem. He started down another aisle that smelled sort of like the woods. It was the wood-shaving bedding in the Furry Friends section. "Maybe a hamster," he said.

"Bor-ing," said Sierra.

"How about a gerbil?" asked Monty.

"Audrey said they bite," said Sierra.

Audrey was their stepmom's kid from before she married Dad, which was how they'd gotten a sister who was both new *and* older than them. Suddenly they had two sisters whose names started with *A*. Audrey, their big sister, and Aisha, their little sister. Monty was the one who'd come up with their nicknames, (which he and Sierra carefully used only with each other): Big A and Little A.

Monty *had* been bit by a gerbil once. He moved on to the guinea pigs. There were brown ones and white-with-black-spots ones. They reminded Monty of cows.

"Reep! Reep! Reep!" cried the guinea pigs.

"I could get a guinea pig," said Monty, trying the idea.

"Nah," said Sierra. "Sounds like Little A when she's mad."

Monty thought the guinea pig was kind of cute. "I can if I want," he objected. "It's my decision!"

"No kidding," said Sierra. "So make it." She skipped off.

Sierra never had trouble making up her mind. She'd made up her mind when she was about two that all she wanted to do was kick around a soccer ball, and she'd never changed it. Their mom called Sierra focused. Their dad called her serious. Monty *wanted* to make up his mind, but it was hard. He had to try out all the choices in his mind for a little while.

Except his "little while" always seemed like a long while to everybody else.

Monty looked up and saw his dad pacing down the Furry Friends aisle. Monty's dad was tall and bald—sort of. He actually had some hair, but so little he figured he might as well go for the shaved-head look. If he was going to go bald, he'd do it pronto.

"How we doing?" he asked, rubbing his bald head like it was a magic lantern and he was hoping a jinni would emerge and grant him his wish: for Monty to be a mind-maker-upper and make up his mind *now*.

Monty saw something that looked like a giant silver-gray mouse. "Can I have one of those?"

"Chinchilla," said his father, reading the sign. "A hundred and ninety-nine dollars! For a big mouse? Sorry, that's too much." He looked at his watch. "Montana," he said in a warning voice, "while we're young, please?"

Montana was Monty's whole name. The story was that the doctor told his mom she was having twins:

two girls. His mom and dad had picked out the names Sierra and Montana. It turned out that the doctor was right about them being twins, but wrong about the two girls part. When they were born, they were a boy and a girl. Apparently his mom decided that Montana would be just as good as a boy's name. Lots of names could be for either girls or boys. Like Brett. Dylan. Logan. Why not Montana? She liked the name and she didn't want to change. Now Monty had to go through life with what was basically a girl's name. He thought this was one situation where changing your mind would have been the right thing to do.

The puppies barked and the guinea pigs reeped. Monty kept looking. The chinchilla was cool. Maybe he should ask his dad if he could have one if he bought it with his own money. But he didn't have that much money and earning it would take time. Maybe he should look at the birds again. Quickly, he ran back to the bird room, pushed opened the heavy door, and slipped inside.

It was extra-warm in there, like a tropical jungle, and extra-noisy, too. Some cages had about twenty tiny birds in them. Finches or parakeets. Other cages had a single big parrot sitting on a perch, like a king on his throne.

Monty stopped in front of a greenwing macaw. Its body was bright red and its wings were blue and green. The pet store guy had said a macaw could take off your finger with its beak. What if he had a bird that bit off the finger of anybody who tried to hold it that wasn't him? That'd be cool. Plus, they lived a really long time, almost a hundred years. If he got the macaw he'd never have to make a decision again about what pet to choose. He'd be set for life.

Monty checked out the price tag: a thousand dollars. Same problem as the chinchilla, only worse. And he didn't want one of the little parakeets. Never mind birds. Monty left the bird room and went back to Furry Friends. He was standing in front of a big glass box full of mice, wondering if he should get a mouse just to save it from being snake food, when Sierra raced toward him in her red socks and red shorts and red shirt, like a fire engine hurtling toward an emergency.

"Dad says if you haven't decided by now it's too late!"

Monty felt the it's-too-late alarm clock go off inside him. As soon as people started getting mad that he was taking too long to make up his mind, it was like his whole heart turned into an alarm clock, screeching *too late! Too late!* Here came his dad, striding down the aisle, tapping his watch to show that time was passing. "Hey, guy," he said, "if you're not really sure what you want, maybe we should wait and see. We can come back another day."

Monty didn't get why grown-ups not deciding something was called waiting and seeing, and was a good thing, but him not deciding something was being indecisive. "Just five more minutes," he said.

Monty's dad took a slow breath and put his I'm-Being-a-Patient-Dad look on his face, which always made the alarm clock in Monty's heart scream a little louder. "Do you have any idea how long we've been in the Pet Emporium?"

Monty shrugged. "Ten minutes?"

"An hour," said his dad. "Do you know what that means?"

Was this some kind of trick question? What did an hour *mean*? Monty knew how much his dad charged people for every hour he spent painting their houses. Was that what his dad meant? "Twenty-five dollars?"

His dad sighed and shook his bald head. "I meant that Sierra's coach isn't going to wait for you to make up your mind. We have to go. *Now*. I'm sorry, but this is nonnegotiable."

"Can we still get doughnuts?" asked Sierra, who had a wicked sweet tooth.

"Maybe," said his dad. "If we can leave *right now*."

"Monty, come *on*," she coaxed. "I'll go halvesies."

Monty was tempted. Doughnuts were good. Their dad didn't usually buy them doughnuts, and normally Monty didn't turn the offer down. And Sierra was always nice about splitting half and half, so he didn't have to choose just one flavor.

"Okay," he agreed. "I guess."

"All right then," said his dad, "sounds like a plan. Let's go."

Wait a second. Going home without a pet today might mean never getting one. There was no way Mrs. Tuttle wasn't going to get in touch with his parents pretty soon. If she didn't call home she'd at least bring up the problem during fall conferences. "Dad, wait a sec!" said Monty. "I don't want to come back. I want to get a pet today."

"Can we still get doughnuts?" demanded Sierra.

"I said 'maybe,'" said their dad.

But it sounded more like a probably-not "maybe" than a probably-yes, and Sierra turned to Monty with an angry look. "Monty, come *on*," she hissed. "Don't do that!"

"Do what?" he demanded. Even though he knew exactly what: changing his mind.

"Don't go back on what you said!"

"I'm not *going back*," he objected. "I changed my mind, is all. So what?"

"But you *said*," she spluttered. "You said you wanted to."

"It wasn't like a promise!" he objected. "Saying okay doesn't mean I promised."

"Enough, you two!" snapped their dad. "Sierra, don't make a mountain out of a molehill. Just drop it already. And Monty, you're making people crazy. Don't say one thing and then ten seconds later say something else. Just make up your mind, all right?"

Monty took a step back. "I did!" he said. "I know what I want!"

"Really?" Monty's dad gave him a skeptical look. "You decided? What did you pick?"

Monty turned his head to see what was in the next big glass box. "A rat," he said.

"A rat?" asked his dad.

"A *rat*?" asked Sierra, making a face. "Mom's not going to like that."

Monty knew that was true. But it was double true that his dad wasn't going to let him change his mind. It was the rat, or nothing. "A rat," he repeated. "I want a rat."

"You sure about this?" asked his dad. "You really and truly want a rat?"

"It's nonnegotiable," said Monty, nodding. "I want a rat."

EAGLE
EYES

Monty could not believe what a lucky pick he had made. The rat didn't bite, and it didn't mind being held. It would even perch on Monty's shoulder while he walked around the house. It was like he could *feel* the rat using its tail for balance. That was so cool. He wondered how it felt to be carried around up in the air, like when someone scored the winning goal in a game and got lifted up by the other players. But that would never happen to him. Sports was Sierra's thing.

"Monty!" said Mrs. Tuttle. "Where are you?"

Trick question. It was Monday morning, and he was in Mrs. Tuttle's fourth-grade classroom, which was in Casco Elementary School, which was in Portland, Maine. But he knew that wasn't what his teacher meant. She meant, *pay attention*. He tried to put a paying-attention look on his face.

Monty's teacher was so little she was hardly taller than the biggest kids. She always told them that she might be small in stature, but her standards were high. She was big on manners; she was big on hand-writing; she was big on . . . everything. She also had super-long hair. It made Monty think of the fairy tale where the girl in the tower let her hair down, and the prince climbed up it every night until the witch found out and got mad—

"Monty!" said Mrs. Tuttle. "Are you listening?"

Another trick question. Was he listening right *now*? Or had he been listening to whatever she'd been saying the second *before*? From the look on her face, probably not.

"Sorry," he said. "I am now."

"Take out your Writer's Notebook, like everyone else has done already," she said. "You're going to write about your neighborhood. You can write about your neighbors, or things you see in the neighborhood. And remember," she raised her voice, "we're using *action verbs*! And *details*!"

The neighborhood. No problem, right? October in Maine meant trees turning orange. Plus his dad was growing a big pumpkin for a jack-o-lantern for Halloween. Monty started writing about all the orange things in his neighborhood.

Wait a second. Orange things was sort of a stupid idea, but the pumpkin had given him another idea. What he really wanted to write about was trick-or-treating in his neighborhood. Families came there specially because the houses were so close together. Halloween in his neighborhood was definitely a better topic. And he figured it was no big deal to start over, since he only had one sentence. He erased what he'd written.

Halloween. Monty wrote a couple of sentences, and then he blanked. He couldn't think of anything else to say. Maybe he needed a new idea. Then he had one. It was perfect. It was the most perfect idea he'd ever had. He could write about this for a whole page! His topic would be the neighborhood's newest resident—his rat. Quickly he tried erasing what he'd already written. Hurry! The words on the paper were his enemy. The eraser was his sword. Kill the words!

The problem was, it wasn't working. He was trying to kill the words so he could start over, but actually he was making a gigantic smudgy mess. He tried erasing harder, and suddenly his pencil ripped through the paper. Forget it! He threw his pencil.

"Ouch!"

It was Jasmine Raines, who Monty had known ever since kindergarten. She always had about a hundred barrettes in her hair. And she always made a gigantic deal out of things.

"You threw that right in my eye!" she yelled. "That hurt!"

"Sorry!" he said. He really was sorry. He didn't actually like Jasmine Raines, but he would never throw a pencil in her eye on purpose.

"Mrs. Tuttle!" wailed Jasmine. "He threw a pencil at me!"

"I didn't throw it *at* you," argued Monty. "I just threw it. I didn't mean to hit you. I swear."

"Monty," said his teacher. "Are pencils for throwing?"

Monty hated it when teachers asked questions that weren't really questions. He knew pencils weren't for throwing! He wasn't two years old!

"No," he said.

Mrs. Tuttle picked up his Writer's Notebook. Pointing to what used to be a page of white paper but was now more like a gray mess of pulp, she asked, "What happened here?"

Monty shrugged. Mrs. Tuttle knew exactly what had happened! He'd thrown his pencil because the eraser wasn't erasing, and he was trying to erase and start over because he'd changed his mind! Was that a crime? He didn't think so. But Mrs. Tuttle was treating him like some kind of criminal. She told the teacher's aide to stay with the class, and told Jasmine and Monty to come with her. Trotting to keep up, Monty followed as she power walked down the hall, down the stairs, and into the main office.

The school secretary sat at her desk by a giant window overlooking the lobby and the front door. Nobody went in or out of the school without Mrs. Tracy knowing all about it. She reminded Monty of the stories where a troll got to decide who could or couldn't go over his bridge.

Opposite the secretary's desk was a wall lined with little boxes, like a honeycomb, where the teachers got their mail. And just past the mailboxes were three doors leading to three more offices, all for people Monty as a rule tried to avoid: the nurse, the social worker, and the principal. Seeing the nurse usually involved some sort of pain. Seeing the social worker usually meant some sort of problem. Monty'd had to talk to him once, back in kindergarten, and he'd vowed not to land there again. And seeing the principal—that just went against all Monty's principles.

Unfortunately the principal was new this year and apparently she had a philosophy: *Every Child Known.*

She was making it a point to get to know every single kid in school. But Monty had a philosophy, too: *Stay Unknown.* The way he saw it, there were two ways the principal knew you: either you were a goody-good kid, or you were in trouble. He was obviously never going to be one of the star, good kids, so unless he wanted to be in trouble—which he didn't—the safe bet was to stay in the middle. The unknown kids.

Mrs. Tracy looked up and said, "Good morning, Mrs. Tuttle. How can I help?"

"Good morning, Mrs. Tracy," answered Mrs. Tuttle. "Is the nurse in?"

The secretary nodded, and Mrs. Tuttle rapped on one of the three doors of doom: the nurse's door. First she asked the nurse to check Jasmine's eye. Then she asked for a box of Band-Aids.

"Monty, let's step out here where we have more room."

Monty didn't want more room. "More room" was in the main office. He glanced around nervously.

Luckily, the other two doors of doom were closed.

"Monty," said Mrs. Tuttle in a loud, bright voice, "we're going to try something *new*."

She said *new* the way people on television said it. *A new car!* Like new was always better. But Monty knew better—new *wasn't* always better. Sometimes it was awesome—like his new pet! But sometimes it meant a new stepparent or a new sister, or *two* new stepparents and *two* new sisters! Being new wasn't necessarily a good thing. It depended what the new thing was.

Mrs. Tuttle pulled the wrapper off a Band-Aid. The new thing was a Band-Aid?

"Band-Aids?" he asked.

"Let's call them *decision-aids*," she said, sticking three Band-Aids on his arm, between his wrist and his elbow. She had switched to talking in a soft, earnest voice. It was the this-is-for-your-own-good voice, which in Monty's experience was never a good thing. "You know the expression, the grass is always greener on the other side of the fence?"

"Sure," he said. He knew that expression. Mrs. Tuttle explained what it meant anyway.

"It means that some people always think things are better somewhere else. Now, I'm concerned that you think the grass is always greener if you change your mind to some other idea. But sometimes you need to pick an idea and stick with it. You need to stay on your piece of grass."

"Grass," echoed Monty, to show that he was listening. And that was when he felt it. He could *feel* somebody else listening. Watching. Slowly, he peeked over his shoulder.

There was the principal, standing in her open doorway.

Principal Edwards had short, white hair. Yellow glasses—the tiny kind just for reading—perched on the tip of her nose. She wasn't looking through them now, though. She was staring over the yellow rims, straight at Monty.

On the wall above the principal's head hung an American flag, and beside it was a poster of a bald eagle with a white head and yellow beak. And all Monty could think was: eagle! With her white head and yellow glasses, the principal looked almost exactly like the picture of the bald eagle.

Mrs. Tuttle was going on and on about how the Band-Aids were going to help him. "I think sometimes you forget how many times you've changed your mind, and how counterproductive that can be. These are going to work as reminders. When you change your mind, a Band-Aid will come off. It's okay to change your mind once"— she pointed to the first Band-Aid, "or twice"—she pointed to the second Band-Aid. "But when the last Band-Aid comes off, it means you're out of chances. It means changing your mind isn't going to help. Do you understand the plan?"

"The plan," said Monty, nodding. He did understand the plan.

Apparently so did the principal. "That sounds like a very good plan for—who do we have here?"

Mrs. Tuttle nudged him, and he said, "Monty."

"Just Monty?" asked Principal Edwards.

"Montana," he said his whole first name. Then his last. "Greene."

"Well, Mr. Greene, it sounds to me like Mrs. Tuttle has an excellent plan. You don't want to be a waffler, do you?"

"What's a waffler?"

It was Jasmine, standing in the open doorway of the nurse's office.

"And who do we have *here*?" asked the principal.

"This is Jasmine Raines," said Mrs. Tuttle.

Principal Edwards said, "Well, Jasmine, a *waffler* is somebody who *waffles*. They can't make up their mind. They go back and forth from one thing to another, wasting their time and everybody else's." She pointed to the big clock on the wall. "And we don't have time to waste! It's time to be learning! So, Jasmine—Monty—off you go!"

So much for staying unknown. The principal knew exactly who he was now. He was Monty Greene, the waffler.

NUT-FREE LUNCH

Monty made it through the next couple of hours without Mrs. Tuttle feeling the need to rip any decision-aids off his arm, and then—*finally*—it was time for recess. Monty had first recess and second lunch, along with about a hundred other kids. The other half of the school flip-flopped; they had first lunch and second recess. The two groups weren't divided up by age, though. Both had kindergartners through fifth graders, so the older kids could model good behavior for the younger kids.

Monty ran through the doorway that led to the playground, heading as fast as he could go for the farthest-away place he could go: the fence at the edge of the field. This side of the chain-link fence was all grass but the other side, where the mowers didn't mow, was like a jungle of giant weeds. There was bamboo and sumac and long bittersweet vines. A flock of starlings liked to hang around there, perched along the fence top and on the sumac that was turning from green to orange.

When Monty reached the fence he tagged it, like he was safe at home base. The starlings took off in a racket of cawing and beating black wings. From across the playground, he saw Sierra galloping toward him. How come? She usually hung out with friends from her class during recess.

Sierra was in a combined fourth and fifth grade class. Everybody knew that if you were in the younger grade of a mixed-grade class, it meant you were above average. That was Sierra. Monty's class was a straight fourth grade. Everybody knew that being in a plain, single-grade class meant you were just average. That was Monty: just average. Except in changing his mind! If they graded for waffling, he'd be well above average.

Sierra ran up to Monty. "Can I see?" she demanded.

"See what?"

"The Band-Aids! Did the principal really put Band-Aids on you?"

"No—I mean yes, but no!" said Monty, confused. "Not the principal. Mrs. Tuttle. How'd you know?"

Sierra always seemed to know everything. She knew enough to be in the four-five class. She knew that playing soccer was pretty much all she wanted to do, besides get good grades. Now she even knew about the Band-Aids! Sometimes Monty wondered why he had to end up with somebody who knew everything for a twin? And sometimes Monty couldn't help it. Sometimes he hated her.

"How do you think?" asked Sierra. "Jasmine Raines is telling everybody. Remember that time you and Devin got in so much trouble?"

Monty was starting to have a bad feeling in his stomach. A carsick kind of feeling. Except he wasn't even *in* a car. Of course he remembered how much trouble he'd gotten in. How could he forget?

Way back in kindergarten, he and Devin Hightower had gotten hold of a permanent marker and decided to write something on the outside of the school. Monty had picked the word, and Devin had done the actual writing. When word got out who did it, they both had to have a chat with the social worker. Then they had to do an hour of community service, helping the janitor clean classrooms. And finally, the entire school had to go to an assembly with Officer Friendly and Firefighter John on how bad graffiti was. And Jasmine Raines practically got an award for being the whistle-blower.

"What else did she say?" asked Monty.

"She said you stabbed her with a pencil."

"That's not true!" objected Monty.

"Says you," said Sierra.

"Ask anyone!" said Monty. He looked around for somebody to tell Sierra the truth. There was Devin, running past. Monty flagged him down. "Devin! Hey, Devin!"

Devin circled back to the fence. Panting, he stared bug-eyed at Monty. He'd lost so many pairs of eyeglasses that now his mom made him wear them with an elastic around his head. It gave him a sort of mad scientist look, like he wore goggles. "What's up?"

"Tell Sierra I did *not* stab Jasmine Raines with a pencil. It was an accident, right?"

"Totally," agreed Devin. "Who says he stabbed her?"

"Jasmine," said Sierra. "She was the one who told everybody about you guys writing on the school, and now she's telling everybody about the pencil and the Band-Aids."

"Poop," said Devin, cracking up. "We wrote *poop*! We were so little we thought *poop* was a bad word!"

Monty laughed, too, but not for long, because he had to stop laughing and start worrying about Jasmine Raines. "I can't believe Jasmine is telling the whole school," he grumbled.

"Duh," Sierra said, reminding him how stupid he was. "Remember what Mom called her?"

Monty remembered. "The Town Crier," he said.

"The *what*?" asked Devin.

"It's from olden days," explained Sierra. "Like from before they had telephones or television. Somebody walked around shouting news and stuff."

"Tell-a-lie," complained Monty. "Get it? Tele-phone, tele-vision, tell-a-*lie*."

"Except it's not a lie," said Sierra. "It's basically true, right?"

"I threw a pencil," admitted Monty. "But not *at* her. She was just in the way."

Sierra shrugged. "Whatever. Everybody knows about the Band-Aids."

"*Decision-aids,* you mean," corrected Devin.

Monty groaned. This was out of control. Apparently Jasmine Raines had told anybody and everybody about the Band-Aids. Correction: decision-aids. So did that mean she was going to tell—*or already had told*—how Principal Edwards warned him not to be a waffler? Monty was definitely feeling carsick now. He wished he could buzz down the window to get some fresh air. Too bad he was already out in the fresh air.

The bell rang. Monty and a hundred other kids scrambled to line up, troop through the double doors and down the hallway, and file into the cafetorium— the big room that doubled as a cafeteria at lunch and an auditorium the rest of the time.

As usual, the cafetorium was crazy crowded and crazy noisy. Monty lost track of Devin and Sierra right away. He got in line and got a carton of plain milk and a slab of pizza. At the end of the line he looked around for a place to sit.

Monty walked by a couple of girls from his class: Emma Robinson and Ella Bakunda. He knew them because they played flute in the band and so did he. (Long story, starting with a clarinet and switching to a way-too-heavy alto sax and ending with his mom and dad saying they weren't going to help him change again, and the band director coming up with an extra instrument—the only way he could stay in the band—a flute.) Ella and Emma were nice enough, but he didn't want to sit with girls.

In the middle of the cafetorium, Monty stood,

holding his lunch tray. By now most kids had taken seats and started eating. Monty was one of the last kids standing. His milk was getting warm and his pizza was getting cold. Still looking around for somewhere to sit, he saw a teacher's aide staring at him. She pointed a finger straight at him and then lowered her hand. *Sit down.* If he didn't take a seat soon she'd be on her way over to yell at him. But where was he supposed to sit? Monty searched, and—finally—saw a space.

Right next to Jasmine Raines.

No way. There was no way he was going to sit with Jasmine Raines, the Town Crier. Cry*baby*, more like it.

Except just then Monty caught a glimpse of something even scarier than the thought of lunch with Jasmine Raines. The something had white hair and yellow glasses. It was Principal Edwards, standing at the edge of the cafetorium, talking to the teacher's aide. She was like a big bird of prey, hovering, and he was . . . the prey. Now the aide was pointing right at him! This was an emergency! Quickly he started to slide onto the end of the bench seat next to Jasmine, but she stopped him.

"Wait!" she yelled.

"What?" objected Monty. "I can sit here if I want."

"What's in your lunch?" she asked.

There was something in Jasmine's voice—like she wasn't kidding—that made Monty pause. In the middle of the table a sign in big block letters read: NUT-FREE TABLE. Monty had heard about the nut-free table. It was for any kid with a nut allergy. Monty didn't have nut allergies, and he didn't have any friends with nut allergies, so he'd never sat there before.

"Montana Greene," said a voice. "Having trouble deciding where to sit?"

Principal Edwards's words felt like talons grabbing him. Why was it that grown-ups always used your whole name when you were in trouble? It was like they were going to cast a spell and they had to use your whole name or it wouldn't work. Or else they called you by your last name, pretending they were treating you like a grown-up, when really they were treating you like a baby.

"No!" he protested. "But there're no seats left!"

"I see a seat," said Principal Edwards, and with a triumphant note in her voice because she had learned the names of not one but two students today, she added, "right next to Jasmine!"

"But I can't sit here, right?" he tried. "Because it's the nut-free table?"

Principal Edwards studied the table. "I see other children here with pizza and milk. Jasmine, is pizza and milk all right at this table?"

"Yes," said Jasmine, nodding. "The lunch lady said it was good."

"Excellent," said Principal Edwards. "From now on, Mr. Greene, consider this your table."

"What?" cried Monty. "But what if I want peanut butter for lunch?"

"You can eat peanut butter at home. This is a simple consequence of your behavior. If you can't make a decision, then someone else will make the decision for you. I made the decision that you will sit here. End of story."

Monty hated it when grown-ups said "end of story." How could it be the end? She didn't mean till the end of the year, did she? Because it was only October!

"For how long?" he demanded.

"Until the end of the year," she said. "Or until you learn to stop waffling. Whichever comes first."

WAFFLES

Monty had no idea how long it would take to prove to Mrs. Tuttle that he didn't need any decision-aids on his arm, and to prove to Principal Edwards that he didn't need to sit at the nut-free table. But he did know how long it would take him to live down his new nickname. Forever.

Back in the fourth-grade room after lunch, the guys got started teasing right away. Tristan Thompson-Brown asked Ethan Ho what he'd had for breakfast. Ethan said waffles and asked Tristan what he'd had. Waffles, declared Tristan. Waffles were his *fave*. Waffles, waffles, waffles, added Devin Hightower, joining the fun. Everybody loves waffles! Even super quiet Lagu Luka, who had just moved here from Sudan, smiled as he learned a great new word.

"Waffles!" he repeated. "I like waffles, too."

"Quit it, you guys," said Monty.

"Quit what?" demanded Tristan.

Tristan Thompson-Brown had the word brown in his name, but his hair wasn't brown. It was orange— the same bright orange as the hats people wore in the woods during hunting season, so nobody would accidentally mistake them for a deer or a moose. It was like his whole head was saying, not me!

"Quit calling me Waffles," said Monty.

"Okay, Waffles," said Tristan.

It was going to be a long day, thought Monty. It was going to be a long year.

"One two three, eyes on me," said Mrs. Tuttle as she grabbed a marker and printed HIDDEN TREA-SURES on the whiteboard in big block letters. It was the name of their new Learning Expedition. They were going to be discovering some treasures hidden "right in plain sight!" And on Wednesday they would kick off their expedition with a field trip.

Monty wondered if Mrs. Tuttle did the slow pull

or the fast pull when she took off a Band-Aid? And how was he supposed to prove to the principal that he wasn't a waffler and could sit wherever he wanted at lunch? He had a lot of questions. Unfortunately, so did Mrs. Tuttle.

"What sort of behavior will I be looking for on Wednesday?"

Ella Bakunda and Emma Robinson both shot their hands up in the air.

Mrs. Tuttle called on Monty. "Monty," she said. "Are you listening?"

The truth was that Monty had been so busy worrying about the waffler thing that he hadn't been listening. But he'd heard the behavior lecture before so many times he couldn't count. He averaged *not this time* together with *a million times.*

"Sort of," he said.

"And what did I just say?"

Emma Robinson had her hand in the air again, but Mrs. Tuttle still wasn't calling on her. She wasn't going to let Monty off that easy. "Monty?"

He could feel the class tuning in. A mini-battle between him and Mrs. Tuttle was more interesting than the usual school stuff.

"Monty? What did I just say about what sort of behavior I expect?"

Why didn't he just give up and admit that he wasn't listening? Because he didn't want Mrs. Tuttle to win! Besides, field trip behavior was a no-brainer.

"Our best?" he tried.

Lagu Luka cracked up, laughing. "Our best behavior!" he blurted.

Mrs. Tuttle fixed a stare of disapproval on Lagu for laughing at Monty's joke, and then on Monty for making it. "Monty, I'd like you to make up your mind to be on your best behavior for the rest of the day, please," she said, and without waiting for him to say anything, she asked everyone to go over to the window and look outside.

"What can you see from our window, right in plain sight?"

From up here on the second floor, Monty could see a lot. The spot where he always hung out at recess, by the chain-link fence. The new "satellite classrooms" stuck on the playground because there wasn't enough room for all the kids this year. The Eastern Promenade, which was the last street before the ocean. Bright orange sumac on the hill that sloped from the Eastern Promenade down to the water. At the bottom of the hill, the huge dome shapes of the sewage-treatment plant. Then the ocean. And out on the ocean, islands. That would be cool, if the field trip was to one of the islands.

Kids were raising their hands and calling out answers to Mrs. Tuttle's question.

"Swings!"

"Trees!"

"There goes a car!"

"The ocean."

Lagu came up beside Monty. "She's *strict!*" he whispered.

Monty didn't want to talk about Mrs. Tuttle. He wanted to make Lagu laugh again. He pointed to the big domes of the sewage-treatment plant. "Maybe our field trip will be there," he whispered. "Hidden Treasures from your toilet!"

"Hidden Treasures!" echoed Lagu with a yelp. "From your toilet!" He clapped his hand to his mouth to hide his laugh.

Tristan Thompson-Brown asked, "Hidden Treasures from *where*?"

A hundred yellow smiley-face barrettes turned toward him. Jasmine Raines was listening.

"Your toilet," said Monty. "I heard our field trip is to the sewage-treatment plant."

"It is not!" objected Jasmine.

Tristan agreed with Jasmine. "No way!"

"Way," said Monty. "Go ahead. Ask."

Monty didn't think Tristan would really do it. Tristan wasn't a get-in-trouble kid. He was the kind of kid teachers sent on errands, like delivering a message to the office. But Tristan called out, "Mrs. Tuttle! Mrs. Tuttle! Is it true our field trip is to the sewage-treatment plant?"

Mrs. Tuttle made a perplexed face. "No," she said. "Who told you that?"

Jasmine Raines raised her hand. "Monty!" she answered. "He said it!"

Tristan explained, "He said it was Hidden Treasures from your toilet!"

"Tristan," said Mrs. Tuttle, raising her voice over the laughter of the entire fourth grade, "that was *not* appropriate. And Monty, did you change your mind again?"

Monty was confused. He didn't think so. "No?" he tried.

She crossed her arms. "Really? You didn't change your mind about being on your best behavior for the afternoon?"

How could he change his mind since he hadn't made it up in the first place? She was the one who had said he should be on his best behavior. That wasn't his decision. He shook his head. No.

"No?" she asked. "Then you didn't make that inappropriate remark?"

"Yes," he admitted, "I did. But"—he stopped, confused. It was true that he'd *made up* the remark, but Tristan was the one who *made* the remark—said it loud enough for everyone to hear. Except somehow teachers looked at Tristan and thought, *not him.* Trouble wasn't his fault. It had to be somebody else's fault. In this case, Monty's. Which seemed totally unfair, but Monty didn't know how to explain all that and besides, he knew it wouldn't matter. Mrs. Tuttle had made up *her* mind that he had changed *his* mind.

"And how are we going to remind you that you've changed your mind *unnecessarily?*" asked Mrs. Tuttle.

Monty hated it when grown-ups asked a question just to make a kid say the answer out loud. He might have to answer, but he wasn't going to say what she wanted him to say. He just held out his arm, and Mrs. Tuttle yanked off a Band-Aid and dropped it in the trash can.

Monty's arm stung a little. One down, two to go. What would happen if Mrs. Tuttle ever pulled off all three? It was like a grown-up counting: *One . . . two . . .* They didn't really want to get to three. They just wanted you to do whatever it was they wanted. *Or else.*

Or else *what?*

MACK

"**Monty, my friend!**" crowed Mr. Milkovich, the bus driver. "How is your day?"

Mr. Milkovich's big hands gripped the steering wheel. He had a big head, too—"for my big brain!" he always said, and then roared with laughter. Monty always tried to sit right behind the driver's seat so he could talk to him. The bus ride was the second best part of his day, with recess coming in first and actual school coming in last.

Monty slid into his usual spot. Somehow he had managed to get through the afternoon without finding out what happened after *or else*. He didn't want to tell Mr. Milkovich about *that*, though. He didn't want to tell Mr. Milkovich about the principal learning exactly who he was, either. Basically, he didn't want to talk about anything that had happened today.

"I got a rat!" he said.

The bus filled up with kids, and Mr. Milkovich pulled out of the bus circle. "Rats?" he asked, heading along the Eastern Promenade. "You got rats?"

"Not *rats*!" explained Monty. "Not like, rats you don't want! Just one rat. He's a pet, and he's totally friendly and nice. He can balance on my shoulder when I walk around. And he has whiskers!"

"Hmm," said Mr. Milkovich, making a thinking-about-it noise. "Does he like apples?"

Mr. Milkovich used to have an apple orchard in the country he came from, before he moved to the United States. Anyone who liked apples was okay in his book.

"I don't know," said Monty. "I'll check it out when I get home."

"Okay," said Mr. Milkovich as he slowed the bus and pulled over to the curb. At the same time, he pushed a button, and the red stop signs on the sides of the bus swung out and its red stoplights started flashing. Monty loved how Mr. Milkovich could stop traffic. Everybody had to stop for a stopped school bus, or else they might get a ticket. Sitting way up high in the driver's seat, Mr. Milkovich was like a king on a throne. King of the road.

A few kids trooped down the aisle and climbed down the big steps and off the bus. A little third grader turned and waved good-bye. "Bye, Mr. Milk," she said, which was what lots of kids called Mr. Milkovich.

"Good-bye!" boomed Mr. Milkovich. "See you tomorrow!"

He drove through the neighborhood, stopping and dropping off kids. At the corner of Washington and Monument Streets he pulled to a stop and a couple of fifth graders shuffled up from the back of the bus. Before they got off, one of them turned to Monty.

"Bye, Waffles!"

"Bye, Waffles," echoed the other kid. "And remember, Waffles, no peanut butter for you!"

Laughing, they sprang off the bus.

Mr. Milkovich turned off the red flashers, pulled in the red stop signs, and kept going on his route. Looking into the big mirror that showed everybody behind him, he asked Monty, "What is it, this *waffles*?"

Monty felt like a flat tire. He was dead. Those kids weren't even in the half of the school he had lunch/recess with. Which meant the entire school had heard what happened.

"It's kind of my new nickname," he explained. "Because the principal called me a waffler."

"The principal is calling you this food of breakfast? Waffles is something you eat, no?"

"Waffles are what you eat, yeah. But *waffler* means somebody who changes their mind too much. She said I shouldn't be a waffler."

From inside Mr. Milkovich came a noise that sounded like the bus was breaking down. "Waff-ler," he grumbled slowly, shaking his big head back and forth. "So this is a bad thing, no?"

"Yep," admitted Monty. "Waffles are good to eat.

But being a waffler is not a good thing. It's bad."

Luckily, Monty's stop was next. Because no matter how much he liked Mr. Milkovich, he didn't want to talk anymore about the meaning of waffler. The bus stop signs swung out, and on the street all the cars slowed down and came to a stop, as if somebody had commanded, *In the name of the king, halt!* When all the traffic had halted, Mr. Milkovich opened the bus door. Monty stood and slung his backpack over his shoulder.

"Mr. Milkovich, my friend," he said, "see you tomorrow."

Mr. Milkovich roared with laughter. "See you tomorrow, my friend."

Monty hopped onto the curb and the bus pulled away. He headed up Atlantic Street, going in and out of the sun as he passed beneath the maple trees' bright orange leaves. Their roots made the brick sidewalk all lumpy and bumpy.

The first thing Monty always did when he got to his dad's house was check out the pumpkin. His dad had planted the seedling right in the compost pile, and now the vine clambered halfway across the back-yard, and the pumpkin was bigger than a basketball. Bigger than a beach ball. It reminded Monty of the story of Jack and the Beanstalk, where the bean plant grew right up into the sky. Just like he always tagged the fence at recess, Monty touched the big orange pumpkin. He was home.

The driveway was empty. No cars. That meant his dad and Beth were still at work. Sierra was at soccer practice. Big A wasn't there, either. Good. He went inside, grabbed an apple, and ran up the stairs.

There was the little guy in his cage. Through the glass, the rat looked at him, and Monty looked back at the rat, with its white fur and brown patches, munching its ratty food. It was so cool the way the rat's paws worked. He could pick up the tiniest seed and hold it while he nibbled. After a while the rat stood up on its hind legs, stretching its whiskery nose toward the cage lid. The guy from the Pet Emporium had given Monty a long lecture about proper animal care, going on and on about how rats were like little Houdinis. They loved to escape from their cage.

Monty unclipped the lid from the cage and lifted out the rat. He bit off a tiny piece of sweet, crunchy apple and held it out. Would the rat eat from his hand? He held perfectly still while the rat looked at the apple, then looked up at Monty. Looked at the apple again and sniffed. And then—yes!—the rat reached out its tiny paws to take the piece of fruit! Victory!

Monty didn't want to make a mistake on something as important as a name—like naming a boy Montana—but he couldn't just keep calling his pet "the rat," either. The rat liked apples. Maybe *apple*? No, that wasn't quite right. How about *McIntosh*? *Mack* for short.

When the apple was all gone the rat—Mack— scritch-scratched his way up Monty's arm, scrambled down his other arm, and came to the two Band-Aids. He sniffed them and looked up at Monty, as if he was asking, *what are these things?*

Monty was glad he didn't have to explain the decision-aids to Mack. He ripped them off—one, ouch! two, ouch!—and threw them on the floor so he wouldn't have to explain them to his dad, either. Unless Sierra told. Or unless Mrs. Tuttle called home. He wondered which house she'd call, if she did call. His dad's or his mom's?

Which reminded him of something he didn't want to think about. Today was Monday. That meant two days to go until Wednesday. Wednesday was Switch Day, when he and Sierra would go to their mom's house. The house where there were already enough creatures, according to his mom.

Monty picked up the rat. "Mack," he said. "We're in trouble, my friend."

HIDDEN TREASURES

The next morning Mrs. Tuttle saw that Monty's arm was bare. She put three new decision-aids on him and pulled one off later when he got up in the middle of Quiet Reading to pick a different book. By Wednesday, Monty knew the drill. He went straight to Mrs. Tuttle's desk, where she said, "Good morning, Monty!" and added as many decision-aids as he needed to start the day with three. After she threw the wrappers in the trash, she clapped her hands.

"One two three, eyes on me!" she chirped. "As you know, today we're kicking off our Learning Expedition. We will be going to Mrs. Calhoun's classroom to meet our Reading Buddies!"

"Mrs. Tuttle, Mrs. Tuttle!" cried Jasmine Raines,

waving her hand back and forth. As usual, she had about a hundred barrettes in her hair. Today they were all butterfly barrettes, which made Monty think of a flower covered with butterflies, like the orange monarchs that had been stopping to feed from the sunflowers in his mom's garden, hurrying south before winter came. Monty had learned all about monarch butterflies in their third-grade Expedition on *Migrations*, which he thought was a way cooler subject than *Hidden Treasures*.

Because it turned out that *Hidden Treasures* was actually just Kindergarten Buddies! And their kick-off field trip was going out to the satellite classroom to meet their Buddies! Monty should have suspected something was wrong when Mrs. Tuttle didn't send them home with permission slips. Because you didn't need a signed note from a parent to walk across the playground! What kind of an Expedition was that? But according to Mrs. Tuttle, there were treasures hidden inside of books and inside of people, too. Their job would be finding the treasure.

"I know a kid in Mrs. Calhoun's class!" said Jasmine. "Can she be my Buddy?"

Mrs. Tuttle shook her head, "I'm sorry, Jasmine. Nobody will choose a Buddy. Those assignments have already been made. Now, we will line up single file. As we walk through the school, our noise level will be *zero*. Let's go."

Monty and his class trooped down the stairs, out through the big double doors, and across the playground. From the outside, a satellite classroom looked a lot like a double-wide trailer, which was what it actually was. But inside, the room looked almost exactly like his old kindergarten.

There was a big *Today Is* sign.

TODAY IS: WEDNESDAY. (If you were student of the day, Monty remembered, you got to change this at morning meeting.)

THE WEATHER IS: SUNNY. (You could change this, too, but only if the weather changed.)

THE SEASON IS: AUTUMN. (This was boring because it only changed four times a year.)

The Next Holiday Is: Columbus Day.

There was also a giant pad of lined paper propped on a big easel, and written on it in were the words: *Today we are going to meet our Big Buddies. Your Buddy wants to learn all about you, and read you a book.*

The kindergartners were so excited they were squirming and wriggling, like the puppies in the Pet Emporium. Monty remembered how excited he was when he got assigned a Reading Buddy, three years ago. They got to go to the library all by themselves to hang out in the Reading Nook and read stories on the beanbags. By now his Big Buddy would be in middle school, in the eighth grade. It was strange to think that he himself had been a Little Buddy once, and now he was a Big Buddy. And someday he would be in the eighth grade.

"Monty," said Mrs. Calhoun. "This is Leo, your Buddy." She spoke in a soft, singsong voice, just like his old kindergarten teacher. "You and Leo may go find a spot to read." She gave him a smile and put Leo's hand in his.

"Monty," said Mrs. Tuttle, in a voice that was not soft. "Make good choices." She gave him a piece of paper for writing down what he learned about his Buddy.

Leo's hand was warm in Monty's. He followed alongside like a little puppy as Monty led the way outside, which turned out to be the best part of the Expedition so far. While the weather was warm, they would be allowed to read outdoors, staying in one corner of the playground where the teachers could see everybody. Monty picked a spot on the top step of the stone amphitheater. On the piece of paper, Mrs. Tuttle had helpfully written a few fill-in-the-blanks. Fill-in-the-blank was boring but easy. The first one was *My Buddy's name is* _____.

"What's your name?" asked Monty.

"Leo!" said the kid with a grin. He had a big smile and big brown eyes, and a buzz cut.

"I know. What's your whole name? Like mine is Montana Greene."

"Leonard Schwarz the third," said Leo. "I can

write it." He grabbed the pencil and paper from Monty and worked until he had written LEON-ARD SCHWARZ III.

"How come you're the third?"

"My dad is Leonard Schwarz Junior and my grandpa is Leonard Schwarz," explained Leo.

"Okay," said Monty. One fact down, four to go. "Do you have any brothers or sisters?"

"One sister," said Leo. "Do you?"

"Three," said Monty. "Sort of." He told Leo all about Sierra, his twin sister, and Audrey, his older stepsister, and Aisha, his baby half-sister.

"You have a lot of sisters," observed Leo.

"Tell me about it," said Monty.

This was turning out better than he had expected. They got to be outside, with no other kids on the playground, and no clouds in the warm, blue sky. And Leo was a pretty funny kid. He complained that his older sister had been in fifth grade last year, and her whole class got lice, and that's why he had to get a buzz cut before he started kindergarten.

Monty read the next fill-in-the-blank out loud: "Pets," he said.

"Do you have a pet?" asked Leo.

Monty forgot that he was supposed to be the one asking the questions. "A rat," he boasted. "I just got him."

"What's his name?"

On Monday Monty had named the rat Mack, but now he wasn't so sure. Looking around, he let his mind float until it bumped into something new. From here he could see the spot on the school where he'd written the word *poop* in black marker. "Officer Rat," he said. "Like a policeman." He told Leo how Officer Rat would eat apples right from his hand.

"Can I see him?" asked Leo. "Can I come over?"

Monty hesitated. He liked Leo just fine. But Kindergarten Buddies was during school. He wasn't sure he wanted to hang out with a little kid after school. "Maybe," he said, not promising.

"When?" pushed Leo.

"I don't know," said Monty. "It's complicated." He

tried to explain that the rat was at his dad's house, but today was the day he and Sierra switched to their mom's after school. So he didn't think he and the rat were even going to be in the same house for a while.

"Why?"

Monty told Leo how he'd known his mom would say no if he asked her for a pet, so he hadn't. He'd asked his dad. Monty knew his dad would say we'll see, then probably, and then yes. His mom had agreed, on one condition: the pet stayed at his dad's house. But somehow, he needed to change his mom's mind.

"How?"

"I don't know," said Monty. "I'm in deep doo-doo, Leo."

"Deep doo-doo!" shrieked Leo. Then tucking his hands under his chin like a begging dog and making a funny face, he suggested, "Do puppy-dog eyes!"

"That's pretty good!" said Monty. He didn't think he could do it as good as Leonard Schwarz the third, but unless Monty came up with a better idea, he might have to go with puppy-dog eyes.

❖ ❖ ❖

By the time school ended Monty hadn't come up with anything better, and he still hadn't by the time the bus glided past his dad's street, or by the time he got off a few streets later at his mom's. He headed around to the back door, where the yellow-headed sunflowers stood guard. Monty picked out a seed and nibbled it. It was pretty cool how the sunflowers' pollen had fed the monarch butterflies, and now their seeds fed the squirrels that climbed up the tall stalks. And him. And he bet the rat would like sunflower seeds, too.

The rat. Time to go inside and beg.

"Mom!" he called out. "Hey, Mom!"

No answer. He saw a note on the fridge: *Monty— I'm working. See you about 4:30.* That meant his mom was here, but he couldn't talk to her. She'd be in the room where she did her massage therapy. Monty wasn't supposed to knock unless it was an emergency. Nobody else was around, either. Bob was still at work, Sierra was at soccer, and Aisha would be with a sitter.

The house was quiet, except for the faint sound of massage music drifting through the walls. It sounded like birds chirping and church bells gonging.

Monty went upstairs. He plunked down on his bed and grabbed a comic book, but he'd already read it. He started a drawing but didn't feel like finishing. He actually took out his homework—math sheets— but he couldn't concentrate. All he wanted was to get this puppy-dog eyes business over with.

Finally he heard a door slam, which meant the client was leaving and his mom was going to pick up Aisha. A little bit later he heard the door again and ran downstairs. There was his mom, holding Aisha. The kitchen smelled like apples. The last time Monty and Sierra were here they'd gone apple picking, and now all the apples were in a big pot on the stove. Monty would rather have a crunchy apple than mushy applesauce any day, but he decided *not* to complain that all the apples were being turned into baby food mush. Not when he was about to beg for mercy.

FLIP-FLOP

"**S**o, Mom," he began.

"Hush, little baby, don't say a word," murmured his mom, singing and swaying back and forth because Aisha was fussing. Pointing to the Band-Aids on Monty's arm, she asked, "What happened here?"

Why did his mom have to notice everything? Especially when she first saw him after he'd been at his dad's. She checked him out from top to bottom.

Monty didn't answer her question because, while she was looking at him, he was looking at her, too. His mom used to have long hair, but when Aisha was born she cut it super-short, saying she didn't want the baby tugging it. Monty still couldn't get used to it. It was like every time he saw his mom, it wasn't *her*. It was some other mom. Once she asked him what was wrong, and he tried to tell her, but she just started talking about *changes*. About Bob and Aisha. But Monty wasn't mad because of Bob, who was pretty nice, or 'cause of Aisha, who was pretty cute, when she wasn't crying. Right now she was old enough to sit up but not old enough to crawl, so lots of times she just sat on her blanket and sucked on a set of plastic cups in rainbow colors. His being mad wasn't about Bob and Aisha. It really was about how his mom just looked . . . wrong. Not like his mom. Like his *not-mom*.

Monty didn't know why he said what he said next. He wanted to be asking about his rat. His mom wanted an answer to her question about the Band-Aids. But instead of doing either of those things he blurted out, "Are you gonna grow your hair back?"

Before his mom could answer, the door opened and in came Sierra in her soccer uniform—red socks, red shorts, and a red shirt with Pronto Painting across the front. Right behind her came Bob, who said in unison with Monty's mom, "No cleats in the house!" Sierra plunked down on the kitchen floor and tugged off her soccer shoes. Bob took off his jacket—underneath he wore a T-shirt that said GOD BLESS EVERYONE. NO EXCEPTIONS.

On days when they stayed here, Bob picked Sierra up from soccer on the way home from his job, which was going around to people's houses fixing their computers. Bob was the kind of guy who, if you were lost and you had to ask somebody for help, you'd ask him. Which actually happened to Monty. He and Sierra and their mom were at the Cumberland Fair, and Monty had spent too long looking at the pigs, which were *gigantic.* Suddenly he realized his mom and Sierra were gone. He went up and down all the livestock barns—more pigs, goats, chickens—and then the boring barns, with skeins of yarn and jars of golden honey, until finally he knew, he wasn't going to find them. His mom had always told him, *if you're lost, find somebody who looks like a grandmother!* But Monty decided to ask for help from the guy standing by the chickens and wearing the NO WORRIES shirt.

That guy was Bob, who took him to the place where lost people found each other, and waited until Monty's mom showed up. After that, he came over a couple weeks later for a thank-you supper. And a couple years after that, he and Monty's mom got married.

"Buh!" squealed Aisha.

Bob picked up a big wooden spoon and began stirring the applesauce, so the smell of apples floated through the kitchen. "You hear that? She said my name! So, what's going on around here?"

"Monty still doesn't like my haircut," said Monty's mom, swaying back and forth the way she did whenever she was holding Aisha. "But I was just going to tell him that when this little gal's not grabbing anymore, I'll probably grow it back."

"Mom," said Monty. He still needed to beg for mercy. "Hey, Mom."

"What about those Band-Aids?" she asked. "Did you hurt yourself?"

Sierra got up off the kitchen floor and opened the fridge. "Mrs. Tuttle's punishing him," she said. "And did you tell her about the rat yet?"

"Sierra!" shouted Monty. He wanted to pound his sister! She was the one being the Town Crier! "Shut up!"

"What?" asked Sierra, as if she was totally innocent. "I'm just *saying*. It's no big deal. Everybody at school knows."

"Knows what?" asked Monty's mom. "Monty, what's going on? Mrs. Tuttle's punishing you because of a rat?"

"No!" shouted Monty.

He was going to keep the Band-Aids a secret, and he was going to beg for mercy about his rat, but now everything was ruined, because Sierra was such a blabbermouth.

"I hate her!" he said, and made a grab for his sister, who scurried behind their mom. They circled around and around. He was yelling and Sierra was yelling and Aisha was crying, louder than both of them.

"Montana! Sierra!" scolded their mom. "Stop it!"

Slowly, Monty and Sierra came to a stop. But Aisha didn't stop crying. Monty's mom handed her to Bob.

"Too much fighting you guys," he said, shaking his head. "Not cool." He took Aisha outside to walk her around the yard.

"Now tell me *what*," said Monty's mom as she turned off the flame beneath the applesauce and put the lid on the pot, "is the matter with you two?"

Monty hated getting lumped together: *you two*. The two of you. As if it was both their faults that they were fighting when it was all Sierra's!

"She started it!" he said.

"I did not!" protested Sierra. "All I said was, did you tell her about the rat?"

Monty's mom made a face like the time Monty stepped in dog doo and she had to help him clean off his sneaker. Like something smelled disgusting. "What *rat?*" she asked.

"His name is Mack," explained Monty.

"Mack?"

"No!" said Monty, remembering. "I changed it. His name is Officer Rat."

"Officer Rat?" asked his mom, still making the bad-smell face. "Where on earth did you get a rat?"

"At the Pet Emporium," volunteered Sierra. "He couldn't make up his mind and Dad said he was out of time, so he got a rat."

"Shut up!" said Monty. "That's not true!" Even though it was true, he didn't want the rat to be known as the pet he got because he couldn't make up his mind. Officer Rat was awesome.

His mom sighed, "Sierra, I want to hear from Monty right now. You can go out in the yard or up to your room."

Sierra made a big show of leaving, stomping loudly up the stairs.

His mom sat down at the kitchen table, cluttered

with newspapers and her laptop and a bowl full of yellow and orange gourds in crazy shapes. "Come and sit," she said, patting the chair beside her. "Tell me."

"Mom, I'm sorry! I know you said no pets! I thought he could stay at Dad's—which was sort of stupid, 'cause a week's too long to leave him there all alone—so could I please bring him over here? Please say yes!"

Monty's mom didn't say yes but she didn't say no, either. She said, "Let me think about that for a minute. What about Mrs. Tuttle? Are you in trouble?"

"Kind of sort of a little," he explained.

"Meaning?"

"Mrs. Tuttle put three Band-Aids on my arm."

"What?" Now Monty's mom had a puzzled look on her face. "Why?"

He was doomed. She could eke the story out of him bit by bit—kind of like doing the slow pull with a Band-Aid. Or he could tell the whole story all at once—kind of like the fast pull. He picked the quick way.

The story came tumbling out: the writing assignment; how he got a better idea so he tried to start over but his eraser ripped his paper; how he threw his pencil but he didn't mean to hit Jasmine; and how now Mrs. Tuttle put three Band-Aids on his arm every day, and every time he changed his mind, she pulled one off as a reminder. "She calls them decision-aids," he said. "I hate her!" Monty felt so mad, he couldn't stop. "And I hate Sierra, too!" he added.

Monty knew what would happen now. His mom would give him a lecture about how *hate* was a very strong word, and didn't he actually mean he was *very angry*? And Sierra wouldn't get in trouble at all.

But his mom didn't give that lecture. "I don't think I like the sound of this," she said as she pulled over her laptop. "I'm going to write Mrs. Tuttle and set up a time to speak with her."

"Mom, no!" cried Monty. "You can't!"

"What do you mean, I can't? Of course I can talk with your teacher."

How could his mom not know what a disaster talking to his teacher would be? Mrs. Tuttle would be mad because he had tattled on her. She'd take it out on him in a hundred little ways for the rest of the year.

"Just—no," he spluttered. "It's just, like, temporary. I think it's only for the week, or something. Mom, I'm handling it. *Please*."

Monty hoped that adding *or something* made what he said not a lie. Besides, Mrs. Tuttle never said anything about how long it would be. Maybe it really was temporary!

"Okay," said his mom with a sigh. "I'll wait on that. But Monty, there's something I want you to think about for me, okay?" She took hold of his hands. "I haven't made a decision yet, but something I'm thinking about—and I'm asking you and Sierra to think about this, too—is having the two of you flip-flop."

Monty's nose was starting to itch. He needed to scratch wicked bad. Finally he had to let go of his mom's hands and scratch his nose. His fingers smelled like the oil she used for her last massage. Peppermint.

"Flip-flop?" he asked.

"Instead of both of you going to dad's together and both of you coming here together, one of you would be at dad's while the other one was here, and vice versa. You two could . . . take a little break from each other."

It was true Monty got really mad at Sierra sometimes. She bugged him a lot—like today—and when she bugged him, they fought. But that was no big deal. All kids fought, right? It was no bigger a deal than scratching an itch. Thinking about scratching made his nose itch again. He peppermint scratched some more, trying to imagine being here without his sister. Or being without her at Dad's. It was hard to imagine. No matter how much he hated it when his mom said *you two*, the two of them had always been together. What would it be like if they weren't?

Maybe they wouldn't be lumped together so much.

Lumping was one of the bad things about being a twin. If something one twin did made Mom or Dad mad, the other twin could pay the price. Because a mad-at-one-twin parent was a grumpy-with-the-other-twin parent. It was grumpy lumping, and it wasn't fair.

But being a twin had tons of perks, too. Both his mom and dad kept pestering Monty to invite a friend over once in a while, but he hardly ever bothered. Because Sierra was always there. Or if she wasn't there right that second because she was at soccer, she'd be home soon. Monty liked always having somebody to hang out with.

Basically, there were good and bad things about being a twin. Flip-flopping would mean getting away from the bad stuff, like grumpy lumping. So maybe he should say yes. But flip-flopping also meant losing the good stuff. So maybe he should say no.

"Do I have to decide right now?"

His mom frowned, but before she could start a lecture on how he should just say his gut feeling and not worry about his answer being set in stone, the telephone rang. She glanced at the caller ID. "Schwarz," she said, not picking up.

Schwarz? Schwarz! Leonard Schwarz the third! Leo!

"That's my new Buddy!" said Monty.

"A friend?" His mom snatched up the phone. "Hello?"

For a little while she listened, nodding, then said, "Just a second. I'll check with Monty." She held the phone down. "Honey, Mrs. Schwarz says Leo wants to come over, if that's okay with you. She says Saturday is good for him." She was giving him a big say-yes smile. "That's good for you, right?"

"Uh," said Monty, blanking. "I don't know."

"I thought you said he was a new friend?"

Monty felt his heart pick up speed, like an electric fan that somebody had turned on. "Kind of," he answered. Buddy was a word for friend. Kindergartners were new in a way, at school.

"Monty," said his mom in a whisper, so Mrs.

Schwarz wouldn't hear, "it's not a big deal. Just say yes or no." Her smile was starting to look tired, like the faces of people who worked in stores who *had* to smile at you. "Leo's mom is waiting, honey."

His mom's words didn't help. They just made Monty feel like somebody had turned up the fan even higher. It was bad enough kids calling him Waffles. What would they say if they knew Monty was hanging out with a kindergartner on the weekend?

But what about his rat? This was too good a chance to pass up.

"He wants to see the rat," said Monty.

"The rat?"

"The whole reason Leo wants to come over is to see my rat," explained Monty. "So can the rat come over while I'm here?"

Monty's mom stared at him, thinking. Trying to make up her mind.

Monty knew that now was the moment. His big chance. He added his best impression of Leo's pleading puppy-dog eyes. "Please?"

THE FIVE FACTS

"Did you get your five facts?" asked Jasmine the next day at the nut-free table. Today the hundred barrettes holding her hair in place were white kitty cats.

"Not exactly," said Monty, unzipping his lunch box.

That morning, Mrs. Tuttle said she hoped they had all done some good "digging for treasure." She hoped they had each gotten at least five facts about their Kindergarten Buddy, because soon they would begin writing their first draft—their sloppy copy—all about their Buddy.

"How many did you get?"

Monty had been so busy telling Leo all about his rat that he hadn't found out if Leo had a pet. He'd been so busy telling Leo about his own sisters that all he knew about Leo's sister was she had lice last year. The only solid fact he knew about Leo was that his whole name was Leonard Schwarz the third.

Monty opened up his milk carton and stuck in a straw. "One, basically," he admitted.

"How are you going to write your sloppy copy?"

Monty figured he could get his facts on Saturday, when Leo came over. Because his mom had said yes to the rat! Bob said he knew a guy who would probably have an extra cage, so last night he and Monty went and picked up the cage and then the rat. The one bad thing was the lid didn't have any clips to keep it on tight. Bob helped him weigh it down with a couple of dictionaries at the corners.

Monty didn't want to explain all this to Jasmine. He wouldn't lie about hanging out with Leo, but he wasn't going to brag about it either. And telling Jasmine, the Town Crier, meant the whole school would know. He just shrugged, as if he didn't know and didn't care.

"Wow," said Jasmine, a big-eyes, big-mouth expression of shock on her face. "You are in so much trouble!"

"Maybe," said Monty, and he turned away, scanning the cafetorium. Right away he saw the guys from his class. Ethan Ho. Lagu Luka, the new kid who laughed at his jokes. Monty's old friend and partner in crime, Devin Hightower, glasses strapped around his head so he wouldn't lose them. And orange-haired Tristan Thompson-Brown, who somehow never got in trouble. How long till Monty could sit with them instead of here at the nut-free table? Monty wanted to be at that other table so bad, he broke a rule. The no shouting from table to table rule.

Waving, he called, "Hey, you guys!"

Tristan must have heard him because he looked Monty's way. "Hey," he shouted, and waved, too. "Hey, Waffles!"

Then Ethan and Lagu and Devin all echoed Tristan.

"Hi, Waffles!"

"Waffles!"

"Waffles, did you have waffles for breakfast?"

"I said, so what are you going to do?" came a voice beside him. "About your five facts?"

Monty didn't answer. He felt all hot and cold at the same time: frozen cold, like he couldn't move; and boiling hot, 'cause he was so mad. Tristan Thompson-Brown was making fun of him, and the other guys were going along. Like it was funny. But it wasn't funny. Not to Monty. He knew what Tristan would say if he asked him not to call him Waffles, though. He'd say, *I was just kidding. Can't you take a joke?* Monty knew that saying something would make it a hundred times worse.

Jasmine kept pestering. "Are you going to tell Mrs. Tuttle?"

"No!" said Monty. "And you better not run and tattle like you always do!"

"I do not!" protested Jasmine.

"You do so!" argued Monty. "You ratted me out—" he started, and then stopped. As he said it, he realized that was being totally rude to his rat. Why did people use the word rat like an insult, anyway? He knew about how some rats were bad—how back in the Middle Ages they had fleas and then the fleas spread diseases—but that didn't mean that all rats were bad. Maybe some were but some—like his—were good.

"You tell on me *all the time*," said Monty.

"Like when?"

"Like when I wrote *poop* on the school! Like when my pencil hit you *by mistake*! Like when Mrs. Tuttle asked who said we were going to the sewage-treatment plant, and you said Monty!"

"I was just *saying*," Jasmine defended herself.

"Well, you should stop saying things that get me in trouble!"

Monty could not believe anyone could be so stupid. Jasmine must be pretending she didn't know that saying certain things to certain grown-ups was going to mean certain trouble for the kid she was *just saying* things about! It was the exact same excuse

Sierra used yesterday after she blabbed everything to their mom. I was *just saying*. In the end, things hadn't turned out too badly. His mom had said yes to the rat. But Monty was still mad at Sierra. Maybe they *should* do that flip-flop thing.

"I'm sorry!" said Jasmine. "I didn't know! Mrs. Tuttle asked a question and I answered, but I wasn't trying to get you in trouble!" She looked like she was about to cry. "I swear!"

When Sierra *just said* things about him, she was definitely trying to get him in trouble. But maybe Jasmine wasn't. She looked so upset that Monty wondered if he should believe her. Believe her or not, he knew what would happen if Jasmine actually did cry. More trouble for him.

"I'm really sorry," she said again.

"Okay, okay," he said. "Chill. You can owe me, all right?" He picked his tuna roll-up from his lunch box. "What you got?"

Jasmine smiled and held up a rolled-up sandwich. "Turkey tortilla!" she said, which seemed to be a signal for all the other kids at the nut-free table to start sharing the contents of their lunches.

"I've got yogurt," announced Katy.

"Me, too," said Kelsey. She turned to Kieran and commanded, "Don't say it!"

Kieran said it anyway. "Me, three!" she announced, giggling and spooning up a big gloppy spoonful of yogurt.

"You're not three," contradicted Kelsey. "You're five. Five years old."

Kieran's laughing face crumpled, as if she was about to cry. "But I have yo-gurt! And one and two and three!"

Kieran and Kelsey and Katy were like the nut-free family. Katy was a fifth-grader in Sierra's four-five class, Kelsey was in third grade, and Kieran was in Mrs. Calhoun's kindergarten. The two older girls had long ponytails of light brown hair, and Kieran had two light brown pigtails. The other nut-free kid was Sam, who said, "We get it, Kieran. You're the third person who has yogurt. You, three! We get it!"

Sam was in third grade, a year behind Monty. He played soccer, so Monty had seen him around at the tournaments his dad made him go to sometimes, to show support for Sierra. Monty figured he better show some support now for Sam's anti-crying effort. There was way too much almost-crying going on here at the nut-free table.

"We get it, Kieran!" he echoed. "You have yogurt. That's cool." Hoping to get her off the yogurt subject, he asked, "So, who did you get for a Big Buddy?"

Monty's words did the exact opposite of what he wanted. Tears started streaming from Kieran's blue eyes.

"Good one," said Katy, the oldest sister.

"What?" demanded Monty. "I was just trying to be nice!"

"She didn't get a Big Buddy," said Kelsey, the middle sister.

"And she's bummed," said Katy, which Monty thought was pretty obvious. Kieran's tiny kindergarten face was sopping wet.

Jasmine explained. She had tried to get Kieran for a Little Buddy, but Mrs. Tuttle said no, because the Hidden Treasures Reading Buddy Expedition took place on Wednesday mornings. And Mrs. Calhoun said that on Wednesday mornings Kieran met with the speech therapist. The therapist's schedule was completely full so there was no changing Kieran's time. And it was too important to miss.

Sometimes Monty could not believe how unfair teachers could be. "More important than Reading Buddies?" he demanded. "No way!"

"Way," contradicted Jasmine, shaking her white kitty-cat head. "That's what Mrs. Tuttle said Mrs. Calhoun said."

"So she doesn't get a Big Buddy at all?" asked Monty. "That's so stupid! That was, like, the best part of kindergarten!"

Kieran tried to say something, but she couldn't get out more than "I—I—I." Her little kindergarten chest was heaving up and down with her sobs.

Monty didn't blame Kieran for crying, but if she got any louder, he knew what would happen: the teacher's aide would hurry over. And he knew exactly who she would blame: him.

Monty held out his paper napkin. "Kieran, tell you what," he said. "I have an idea. But you gotta stop crying so you can hear me, right?"

Kieran took the napkin. Smearing her tears all over her face, she sniffed a giant sniff. Smiled a tiny smile. "What?" she asked.

"I'll be your Buddy."

It felt like when Mr. Milkovich made the red lights flash and the stop signs pull out on the sides of the bus. *In the name of the king, halt!* Everything stopped. Everyone was looking at him, like he was king of the nut-free table. Jasmine and Sam. Katy and Kelsey. And tiny Kieran with a huge smile on her face.

"You're my Buddy?"

"Leo's my official Buddy, but you can be my *unof-*

ficial Buddy," he explained, trying to say "unofficial" as if it was something special. "Just for fun, okay? Not for real."

Still sniffling, Kieran gave him back the tear-smeared napkin. "When?" she asked.

"Tomorrow," he said. "Recess."

"Promise?" she asked.

"Promise," he said.

Jasmine tried to say, "But Mrs. Tuttle said we weren't allowed"— but Monty cut her off.

"That's not fair and you know it!" he hissed. "And you owe me, so you better not tell!"

"I won't!" protested Jasmine. "I would never do that!"

Monty stuck the crumpled napkin in his lunch box. He didn't feel too good about a promise from Jasmine Raines, the Town Crier, insisting that she would never tell something. He felt more like . . . doomed.

THE KING OF KINDERGARTEN

The next day at recess Monty leaned against the chain-link fence, bouncing—*boing, boing, boing*—with a tiny book in his back pocket. Overhead, the wind was pushing big white clouds across the blue sky. Across the playground Jasmine Raines was marching toward him, holding the hand of a little girl with light brown pigtails. Kieran. Beside them came Lagu, leading a little girl who looked a lot like him, with black hair in braided pigtails. Who was that?

The two big kids and two little kids reached the fence.

"This is my sister, Winnie," Lagu said to Monty. To the little girl he said, "This is my friend, Monty. He can be your Buddy!"

"I can *what?*" demanded Monty.

Jasmine's head today was dotted with the smiley-face barrettes, and she had a big, proud smile on her face, too, as if she'd done something really great. "I told him you were going to be Kieran's unofficial Buddy," she explained. "And he said his sister was in Mrs. Calhoun's class, too. And she needed a Buddy, too, because she has English Language Learners help during Reading Buddies."

"I told you not to tell anybody!" said Monty.

"I thought you meant teachers!" said Jasmine.

"I meant anybody!" shouted Monty. "You didn't tell anybody else, did you?"

"Hardly anybody," cried Jasmine, with a scared look on her face. "Just one other kid."

"Who?" demanded Monty, but the answer was galloping toward him, kicking a soccer ball on the way: Sierra.

His sister came to a stop, panting for breath. "Is it true?" she asked.

"Is what true?"

"About all the Buddies?"

"No!" blurted Monty.

Kieran wailed, "But you *promised*!"

"I know," Monty assured her. "I will."

He *had* promised Kieran, but he hadn't promised this Winnie kid. He turned to Lagu. "Why can't you be her Buddy?"

"She doesn't want me," said Lagu, shaking his head. "I'm her brother."

Monty turned to Jasmine. "Why can't you be her Buddy?"

Jasmine just shook her head, with the same frightened look on her face. Monty couldn't believe this! Jasmine wanted him to do something she was too afraid to do!

Monty was feeling about ten different kinds of mad. He felt mad at Jasmine for blabbing, and for not being willing to be an unofficial Buddy herself. He felt mad at Lagu for going around calling him

Waffles, and then asking for a big favor. How unfair was that? And he felt mad at the teachers for thinking that some kids had more important things to do than Reading Buddies. The only people Monty wasn't mad at were the kindergartners. Kieran, the littlest nut-free sister. And Winnie Luka, who had just moved here from across the world, and who asked him, plainly, "Will you be my Buddy?"

Kieran tried helping her out. "Unofficially," she said. "Not for real."

"Okay, okay," said Monty. He sat down cross-legged on the grass. "But remember, Leo's my official Buddy. Where is he, anyway?"

Kieran plunked herself down beside him. "He's not in school today."

"Absent," said Winnie, sitting down on his other side.

Jasmine and Lagu and Sierra sat down, too. Great, thought Monty. Everybody was waiting to hear a story—his sister, two unofficial kindergarten Buddies, and two—what? Monty didn't know what to call Jasmine and Lagu. Friends? Except friends didn't blab. Friends didn't call names.

"Read!" commanded Kieran.

"Read!" echoed Winnie.

From his back pocket Monty pulled out the book he had brought, but he didn't get any further than the title, *"Chicken Soup with Rice,"* when the fence he was leaning against started shaking. A kid was walking toward them, banging a stick against the fence. Step and *bang.* Step and *bang.* Step and *bang, bang, bang.* It looked like he was walking all the way around the edge of the playground. In a few seconds he had reached the place where Monty was sitting, with Kieran and Winnie and Jasmine and Lagu and Sierra in a semicircle around him. The kid had curly blond hair and a Band-Aid arching across his nose.

"Hi, Finn," said Kieran.

"Hi, Finn," said Winnie.

The curly-headed kid called Finn didn't answer. He just hit the fence with the stick again.

"Can you go around?" asked Monty. "Please?"

Finn didn't say yes and he didn't say no. Monty didn't know what to do. Maybe he should just move and let the kid go by?

"Finn's in our class," said Kieran.

"He didn't get a Buddy, either," said Winnie.

"How come?" asked Monty.

Nobody answered. The girls didn't know where Finn had been during Reading Buddies, and Finn wasn't saying. Monty figured that wherever Finn was being sent for extra help, it wasn't anywhere fun. Extra help usually wasn't. For a minute, Monty went back and forth, trying to decide what to do.

The last thing he needed was another Kindergarten Buddy.

But how much harder could it be, reading to three kids than two?

A lot harder, maybe. Finn didn't look like the kind of kid teachers called *cooperators*. He looked more like he was ready for a fight.

But it would be mean to leave him out, and Monty wasn't into being mean. He knew how that felt.

"Here's the deal," he said. "Leo's my official Buddy, but these guys are my unofficial Buddies, and you can be, too. Want to?"

Silently, Finn dropped his stick and plopped down on the grass, and Monty began reading.

"'In January it's so nice
While slipping on the sliding ice,
To sip hot chicken soup with rice.
Sipping once, sipping twice,
Sipping chicken soup with rice.'"

He knew the rhyme by heart, so while he read the words out loud he could think about other things. Like how he'd felt like such a bigshot king when he offered to be Kieran's Buddy. He wasn't feeling much like a king anymore, unless king of kindergartners counted. He was feeling more like a guy with three extra reasons why Mrs. Tuttle was going to be mad at him. And three reasons why Leo was going to be—what? Would Leo be mad, too? And what was Monty's mom going to say when she saw that his "buddy" was five years old? At least Monty didn't have long to wait. His playdate with Leo was tomorrow.

Saturday morning at his mom's house meant pancakes. Bob was making the pancakes. Monty's mom was putting plates and forks and a big jug of maple syrup on the table. Sierra was sitting on a blanket with Aisha, who was playing with her plastic rainbow cups. And Monty was hanging out with the rat perched on his shoulder, when there was a knock on the door.

Monty's mom said, "You get it, Monty. That must be your friend!" She said *friend* as if it was something wonderful. Like *sunshine*. Or *ice cream*.

Monty opened the door and Leo bounded in wearing light-up sneakers that flashed on and off with every step. From his flashing sneakers up to the top of his buzz-cut head, he was bouncing up and down. "Can I hold the rat? Can I hold the rat? Can I hold the rat?"

Monty's mom made about three different faces

in three seconds. First she looked surprised. Then confused. Then, shaking her head, she gave Monty a smile and an *Oh, well* shrug. "Hello, Leo," she said. "Would you like some pancakes?"

"Sure!" said Leo, bouncing.

Monty grinned. His mom wasn't mad! Problem solved!

Except he still had an even bigger problem. He had to tell Leo about the extra Buddies.

"Buh!" crowed Aisha as she slid the orange cup into the yellow one.

"Good job!" said Sierra. Sierra, who had blabbed to their mom about the rat and the decision-aids. What if she told Leo? Monty couldn't let that happen. He had to be the one. But how? He was trying to figure out what to say and when to say it, when the rat decided to travel from one shoulder to the other. Monty loved how he could feel the rat's feet gripping him. The rat's feet sort of tickled, and sort of scratched, and somehow sort of made Monty feel better. Like he could say what he had to say.

"Let's go outside," he said. "We can feed the rat some sunflower seeds."

"Pancakes ready in five minutes," said Bob.

"And no rat at the table," said Monty's mom.

"We'll be right back," promised Monty.

Outside, the sun was shining on the sunflowers. Gently, Monty pried the rat from his shoulder and placed it in Leo's hands. Then he dug a few seeds from the big face of a sunflower and handed one to the rat. As Leo held the rat in his cupped hands, the rat took the seed in his paws and started to nibble it.

"He likes it!" said Leo, a note of awe in his voice.

"Hey, Leo," said Monty. "I gotta tell you something. Did you know not everybody in your class got a Reading Buddy?"

"They didn't?"

Monty shook his head. "No."

"Who?"

"Winnie Luka. Her big brother is in my class. And Kieran. She sits at the nut-free table. And some kid named Finn."

"Give him another seed!" commanded Leo.

Monty gave the rat a second seed. "And you know how you were absent yesterday?"

Leo nodded. "I threw up," he explained.

"Well, I kind of read them a book during recess."

"He wants another one," said Leo.

Monty gave the rat a third sunflower seed. He wasn't sure if Leo understood what he was saying. This was like the slow pull or the fast pull on the Band-Aid. Maybe it was better to get it over with. "And I kind of told them that I could be, like, their unofficial Buddy," he blurted.

"I'm your Buddy!" insisted Leo.

"You are totally my real, official Buddy," said Monty, hoping Leo wasn't going to freak.

For a second, Leo studied Monty with his big brown eyes. Finally, he echoed, "Your *official* Buddy," as if he liked the sound of it.

"Totally," said Monty.

Leo thought for a while. "I'm the only one who can come to your house," he bargained.

No problem. Monty could agree to that, if it would keep Leo from freaking. "Only you can come to my house," vowed Monty. "You're the only one."

Leo added a final rule. "Only I can hold the rat."

"Right," agreed Monty. "Because the rat's at my house."

Leo nodded. They had a deal. And by the end of the morning, Monty had his five facts.

One (which he already knew): Leo's whole name was Leonard Schwarz the third. Two: Leo had one sister (who had lice last year) and her name was Harriet. Three: Leo and Harriet had a golden retriever named Noodle. Four: Leo's favorite food was pizza and his favorite dessert was apple pie. Five: Leo was a Little Lion Scout, and next month his Scout troop was marching in the parade. And he wanted Monty to come and watch.

"Sure," said Monty.

"Promise?" asked Leo. "Definitely you promise?"

Why did kindergartners want to promise all the time? He had promised Kieran he'd be her Buddy, and then wound up with Winnie and Finn, too. Promises could be dangerous. But Leo had been a pretty good sport, and Monty figured he owed him.

"Definitely, absolutely, positively promise," said Monty. "I'll be there."

TINY BOOK AFTER TINY BOOK

Armed with his five facts, Monty managed to write his sloppy copy about Leo the next Monday at school. That was the good news. The bad news was that from then on, his whole life started revolving around being a Buddy.

Monty thought Leo had been pretty cool about Kieran and Winnie and Finn. But Leo still had to make sure that the other kids knew that he was the *real* Buddy, and he did this by running out to Monty's spot by the fence just about every day. If Leo saw Monty with Kieran, he showed up. If Leo saw Monty with Winnie, or with Finn, he showed up. And if Leo saw Monty all alone, he showed up, too.

It was all part of the unspoken deal: Leo didn't tell

on him about the extra Buddies, and Monty didn't tell Leo he couldn't hang out. Because the last thing Monty wanted was the teachers finding out. He'd probably be hauled off to the social worker's office. Monty lived in constant fear that Jasmine Raines was going to tell by accident. Somehow she'd managed not to, so far, but Monty figured it was only a matter of time.

In the meantime, he had to keep finding books small enough to fit into his back pocket.

"You want *small* books?" asked Mrs. Harkins, the librarian, who had a streak of purple in her dark brown hair. "Do you mean, short? Not too many pages?"

"I mean, tiny," explained Monty, holding up his hands to show the size he needed.

Mrs. Harkins tilted her purple streak to one side, as if the idea of a fourth grader reading a tiny book made her head hurt. "We do have some tiny books," she said. "But they're mostly picture books. You don't want a chapter book?"

Monty shook his head. "I want little books," he said. "A whole bunch."

Mrs. Harkins still had a puzzled tilt to her purple head, but she found what he wanted. She gave him *Harold and the Purple Crayon*. She gave him *The Little Fur Family* and *The Very Hungry Caterpillar*. Best of all, she showed him about twenty books by the same author, Beatrix Potter. There were books about rabbits and ducks and frogs, and even one about a rat named Samuel Whiskers. Everybody's favorite was still *Chicken Soup*, though.

"'In January it's so nice

While slipping on the sliding ice,

To sip hot chicken soup with rice.'"

The kids liked to chime in. Kieran: Sipping once. Winnie: Sipping twice. Finn: Sipping chicken soup. Leo: with rice!

Monty didn't actually mind hanging out with the kindergartners. They were funny. They thought he was super cool, just because he could read. But hanging out with kindergartners was sort of like sitting at the nut-free table. Monty might as well have hung up a sign on the fence saying big-kid-free zone. After that first day, Sierra and Jasmine and Lagu pretty much left him alone. Sometimes Jasmine showed up to say hi, but then she ran off again. Lagu came over once in a while, but he couldn't sit still and he usually took off halfway through a book to race around with the other fourth-grade guys, who stayed far away, as if they were allergic to little kids. If they did swing by, running in a pack, they shouted "Waffles! Hey, Waffles!"

As Monty worked his way through tiny book after tiny book, the weeds behind the chain-link fence were turning yellow and orange and red. And every Wednesday Monty and his class trooped over to the satellite classroom so they could "search for hidden treasures" with their Reading Buddies. Monty always checked out the changes on the TODAY IS sign.

TODAY IS. This was always followed by WEDNES-DAY. Then came the month, and then a number for the date that got bigger and bigger, until finally the month changed from OCTOBER to NOVEMBER.

THE WEATHER IS. This was followed by SUNNY or CLOUDY or RAINY.

THE SEASON IS. Still AUTUMN.

THE NEXT HOLIDAY IS. The first time they'd visited, the sign said that the next holiday was COLUMBUS DAY. Then it changed to say the next holiday was HALLOWEEN, and orange paper pumpkins spotted the classroom walls. After Halloween the pumpkins came down and up went flags of white paper painted with red stripes, and white stars glued to blue squares. THE NEXT HOLIDAY IS: VETERANS DAY.

The morning of the Veterans Day parade Monty woke to a gray sky. THE WEATHER IS: CLOUDY. He lifted the rat from its cage, settled him on his shoulder, and headed down to the kitchen.

"Mom," said Audrey, his stepsister. Otherwise known as Big A. "Is that, like, allowed?"

Audrey wasn't usually around when Monty and Sierra were, because of the schedule. The week they came to their dad's house was usually the same week she went to stay at her dad's house. But sometimes the schedule got changed around and they ended up in the same house at the same time. Monty wasn't too thrilled when that happened. Audrey acted like being thirteen gave her the right to boss him around. She was constantly telling him what to do. Either that, or telling him about all the terrible things that would happen to him when he got to middle school.

"Well," said Monty's stepmom, Beth, "we haven't really talked about it."

Beth was the exact opposite of the wicked step-mothers in the fairy tales. She didn't order him and Sierra around. If there was some sort of problem, she called a family meeting and asked everyone to be part of the solution. Then she called the solution a "house policy" instead of a rule. Monty couldn't figure out how such a nice mom had got Audrey for a kid.

"Mom, that's disgusting," said Audrey. "It's a rat!"

"He's a pet rat," said Monty. "And for your information, his name is Scratcher!"

Monty's dad came out from behind his newspaper. "I thought his name was Mack."

"He changed it," said Sierra, who was sitting at the kitchen table eating a piece of toast with chocolate spread.

"I thought it was Officer Rat," said Beth. "Wasn't it Officer Rat last time you were here?"

"It was," said Sierra. "But then he changed it again. He's changed it a bunch of times."

"How many?" asked his dad.

"A few," admitted Monty.

"Like, ten," taunted Sierra.

"Not ten!" argued Monty. "Dad, that's a lie!"

"Monty, don't call your sister a liar. Sierra, don't exaggerate."

"I'm not exaggerating!" protested Sierra.

"You are so!" objected Monty.

"Sierra—stop," said their dad. "And Monty, did you ever think about just choosing something and sticking with it?" Without waiting for an answer, he picked up the compost bucket from beside the sink and stepped outside, heading for the compost pile.

"Whatever," said Audrey, launching back into her complaint. "Mom, he touched the rat and now you're going to let him touch all the food in the fridge? And what are you doing with that—whatever it is?" she asked, pointing to a red and yellow scarf her mom was holding.

Monty's stepmom held up the scarf. "Isn't this lovely? One of my clients gave it to me. It's from Sudan."

Beth's job was helping people who just got to the United States find jobs and apartments and get their kids settled in school. Sometimes they gave her fabric from the country they'd come from. She belted the scarf around her waist. "Monty, you do understand that you need to wash your hands after you pick up the rat and before you touch anything in the fridge, right?"

"Right," said Monty. "Absolutely."

With Scratcher perched on his shoulder, he washed his hands. Then, carefully (house policy: Take the piece you want and want the piece you take) he grabbed the topmost apple from the fruit bowl and took a big bite.

"Or any food in the cupboard," commanded Audrey.

Monty didn't like being bossed by Audrey, but he decided not to argue right now. It felt good having the rat ride around on his shoulder. He didn't want Scratcher banished.

"Or any food," he agreed.

He took another bite of sweet, crunchy apple. He could hear the rat sniffing, as if it was thinking, you know I love apples! Monty wanted to give him a piece, but he knew Audrey would freak.

"I think that goes without saying," said Beth. She dunked a tea bag in a mug of hot water. "I'm sure Monty gets the point, Audrey. We'll start with that understanding and if there's a problem, then we'll find a solution."

"Which would be no rat in the kitchen, right?" said Audrey.

"*Audrey*," said her mother—a one-word warning to drop the subject.

"*Mom*," said Audrey—dropping it, but getting in the last word herself.

"What about getting silverware out of the drawer?" asked Sierra. "Doesn't he have to wash his hands before that, too? Or else he'll get rat germs on the spoons!"

Monty had expected grief from Audrey. But now his own sister was against him? Maybe he should tell Beth how Sierra used a spoon to eat chocolate spread straight from the jar! Except he would never tell on her! "Thanks a lot," he muttered as his dad came back inside and set the empty bucket by the sink.

"What?" demanded Sierra. "I'm just saying!"

"Saying what?" asked Monty's dad.

Beth fished the tea bag from her cup. "We were just saying," she said, "that of course Monty will be careful to wash his hands after he touches the rat and before he touches anything in the kitchen. It's a nonissue, so let's move on."

Monty's dad knew how to take a hint from Monty's stepmom. He nodded and moved on. "I'm going to walk down to the parade. Who's coming with me?"

"Not me," said Beth. "I've got loads to do around here."

"Not me," said Audrey, heading into the bathroom where she would probably spend an hour fussing with her long, blond hair.

"Not me," said Sierra.

"Me," said Monty. He had promised Leo he would look for him.

"Okay," said Monty's dad. "You sure?"

"Sure I'm sure," said Monty as the rat clambered from one shoulder to the other.

"Really? You positive?"

"I just said so!"

"Well, I'm just asking! Because sometimes you change your mind."

"Well, sometimes I don't!" objected Monty, feeling the rat's feet tightening its grip, as if it was afraid. He couldn't believe this. His dad was always mad at him for not making up his mind, and now Monty's mind was made up, and it seemed like his dad was mad, anyway! How unfair was that!

"Mostly you do," pointed out Sierra.

"I do not!" said Monty. "That's not true!"

"Is so," said Sierra, shrugging. "But, whatever."

Monty wanted to pound his sister. She sounded exactly like Big A. He also wanted to say that maybe sometimes he had trouble making up his mind in the first place, but it wasn't true that he changed his mind once it was already made up. The trouble came when people wanted him to make up his mind before he was ready. Then sometimes he gave an answer that wasn't really his final answer. But he was so mad he couldn't explain all that. All he could say, stupidly, was, "Not *whatever*!"

"John," said Monty's stepmom. "Why don't you and Monty just go? And maybe later we should all talk about—you know."

"The flip-flop thing?" asked Sierra.

Everybody knew about the flip-flop idea by now. Monty's mom had asked everybody to think about it, and Monty's dad had said he wanted to wait and see. Monty's stepmom and stepdad both said it was up to his mom and dad. And nothing had happened. Except every time he and Sierra had a little fight, the grown-ups sent meaningful glances at each other. They were so obvious they might as well be sailing a paper airplane across the room with a note on it: *What should we do about Monty and Sierra?*

THE WEATHER IS: POURING RAIN

"**Y**es, the flip-flop thing," answered their dad, sounding annoyed. "But not now. I don't want to miss the parade. Come on, Monty—while we're young, please? Put that rat away and let's go."

It wasn't Monty's fault they hadn't left yet!

By now he didn't even want to go to the parade with his dad, but he didn't have much choice. He was going and his dad was going. They were going together. He put the rat back in its cage, and they left the house and walked up Atlantic Street and down Congress Street. At the bottom of the hill they found a spot to wait.

Monty's dad pointed to the patchy gray sky. "Looks like it can't decide whether to rain or not."

"Is that supposed to be funny?" asked Monty.

"It was supposed to be," said his dad, "but I guess it wasn't. Hey, I'm sorry, okay? I'm glad you wanted to come with me."

Monty was still sore. "I promised Leo," he said.

"Who?" asked his dad.

"My Kindergarten Buddy," explained Monty. "Leonard Schwarz." He told his dad all about Leo and his sister named Harriet and his dog named Noodle.

"That's pretty nice of you to come and watch him."

"I guess," said Monty.

His dad might think that Monty was being nice, but the truth was, hanging out with Leo was easier than dealing with the kids in his own grade. Leo thought he was awesome. Leo never called him Waffles.

"Who's he marching with?"

"His Scout troop."

"I was a Scout," said his dad.

"You never told me that," said Monty.

"I didn't get too far," admitted his dad. "But your

granddad did. He went all the way to Eagle Scout."

"He did?" Monty felt like an idiot for not knowing. But his grandfather had died before Monty was born, and his dad hardly ever talked about him.

"He gave me the badge he got when he made Eagle Scout," said his dad, "but I lost it. I wish I'd been able to hang onto that."

A loud noise rumbled overhead.

"Here come the planes!" said his dad, but his voice sounded funny. Tight—like he could hardly get the words out.

Monty glanced up and saw something he suddenly realized he had never seen before. His dad had tears in his eyes. It made Monty feel funny, as if he had seen something he wasn't supposed to. Quickly he looked away—up at the sky where the planes emerged from the clouds, zoomed high above the parade route, and then disappeared. The parade was starting.

One after another, the groups went by. The high school marching band trooped by playing "You're a

Grand Old Flag." Monty wondered if he would still be in the band in high school. He didn't see any guys playing flute, though. How could he talk his parents into letting him switch instruments again?

The band went past, and then came a convertible car with Miss Maine perched above the backseat, smiling and waving. Then came some soldiers in uniforms, marching. First were some men and women, and then some older men, and then a couple of super-old guys. Monty's dad said they were veterans from all the different wars. After the veterans came some clowns, spinning around in little cars, and finally the Scout troops in tan shirts with red kerchiefs around their necks. Monty scanned the group for Leo.

"That's him!" shouted Monty, pointing. "See the little kid with the buzz cut? Leo, hey, Leo!" He was waving like crazy and shouting, but he didn't think Leo could hear. Then a big, booming shout rang out.

"Leo!" roared Monty's dad. "Leo!"

Leo turned, saw Monty, and waved. Monty waved back. He felt his dad put an arm around his shoulders and squeeze him close. Monty didn't dare look up. He was pretty sure his dad was crying again.

They watched the rest of the parade—a group of marchers waving flags with doves, a fire engine, and finally a police car—and then listened to some speeches. Monty didn't feel mad at his dad anymore. He just felt afraid he might make his dad sad again. Monty had known forever that his grandfather was dead, but he'd never realized what that *meant*. Granddad was his dad's *dad*. The way Monty felt, thinking about this stuff, made him understand why his dad never talked about his father.

At the very end, after all the speeches, the trumpet player from the high school band played a song all by himself. The crowd was totally silent while the trumpet notes hung in the sky, and Monty knew what he would pick, if he could ever talk his parents into letting him switch instruments again. The trumpet.

Did he dare ask his dad right now? Making an important request called for good timing. Was this a good time or not? Maybe not, because he'd practically made his dad cry. But maybe yes, because here they were. Together. Monty was hardly ever alone with his dad.

"Dad," began Monty.

"Let's get home," said his dad, setting off through the crowd.

"Dad," tried Monty again, trotting to keep up with his dad's long strides. The gray sky was starting to drizzle and the crowd was quickly thinning, people running to their cars. "Dad, you know the trumpet?"

"What about it?"

That sounded like grumpy-dad. Grumpy-dad walking home in the drizzle that was turning to rain. Maybe this wasn't a good time.

"What?" demanded his dad.

Definitely not a good time. "Nothing," he said.

"*What?*" repeated his dad. "Spit it out, Monty."

"Could I play trumpet?" he asked. "Instead of flute?"

"You want to switch instruments?" asked his dad. "Again?"

"Kind of," admitted Monty.

The sky was spitting rain for real now.

"I don't know, Monty. I'd like you to stick with something for once."

"I want to stick with Band," protested Monty. "But I never really wanted to play flute."

The rain was coming down faster and his dad was walking faster, too. "Switching instruments isn't going to solve anything. Sometimes you just have to stick with something until you get better."

"I'm not trying to solve anything," said Monty. "I just want to play trumpet!"

"I don't know," repeated his dad. "Let me talk to your mom."

Monty didn't bother saying anything else. Monty's dad talking to Monty's mom was code for no. They walked the rest of the way up the hill in silence. By the time they turned onto Atlantic Street it was pouring rain. Monty wished he had never brought up the trumpet subject. The feeling he had when his dad gave him a sideways hug was gone. Now he was mad at his dad again, and his dad was mad at him again, too.

And his dad didn't waste any time changing his mind to be in a good mood. They walked though the back door, and *pronto*, his dad called Sierra into the kitchen. It was time for the talk.

"Your mom and I both think it might be good to try this flip-flop idea—you and Sierra getting a little break from each other—just for a little while. What do you two think?"

Monty didn't need to think. This wasn't something he needed to make up his mind about, like choosing between two flavors of ice cream. It was more like the question, Do you like ice cream? Of course. Do you want to stay with your twin sister? Of course! Sometimes they fought. Who cared? Sometimes he got sick of grown-ups thinking of him as half of *you two*. He was him! But neither of those things meant he didn't want to live with Sierra. What was the point of that? The whole best thing about having a twin was always having somebody around—somebody who understood exactly how annoying it felt to be half of *you two*.

But before he could explain all that, Sierra answered, "I don't care." Those were her exact words. *I don't care.*

She didn't care? If Sierra didn't care about being with him, why should he care about being with her? He was so mad at his sister for agreeing to flip-flop that he suddenly agreed, too.

"I don't care either," he said. "We can flip-flop."

"You sure?" asked his dad. "Because if either of you don't want to, we won't. Even if it's only for a little while, we need everybody on board. So, you're sure you want to?"

The truth was, Monty wasn't sure. He'd only said he wanted to because he was mad. The truth was the exact opposite. The one thing he was sure of was that he *didn't* want to.

"I didn't *say* I wanted to," argued Monty. "I said I

didn't care, but if everybody else wants to, then, fine! Whatever!"

Monty's dad rubbed his smooth head, still shiny from the rain. "Now I'm totally confused," he said. "But it sounds like you don't like the idea. Maybe we should table it for a while."

"Table it?" asked Monty.

"Wait and see," explained his dad.

Sierra groaned, "Maybe he should make up his mind once in a while!"

"*Sierra,*" said their dad.

"*Dad,*" said Sierra, mimicking the warning note in his voice.

Monty was so sick of everybody being mad at him for changing his mind that he pretended he hadn't. That he actually did want to flip-flop. "I made it up!" he blurted, pointing to his twin sister. "I don't want to live with *her.*"

YOU CAN'T CROSS OVER MY BRIDGE

When Monty's class got to the satellite classroom the next morning he saw that Mrs. Calhoun had already changed the TODAY Is sign. Veterans Day had come and gone. Now the sign said THE NEXT HOLIDAY IS: THANKSGIVING. What Monty didn't see was Leo.

"I'm sorry, Monty," said Mrs. Calhoun. "Leo is absent today."

Leo being absent meant that Reading Buddies was pretty boring. But Monty was psyched for circle time. Wednesday afternoon circle was for talking about the Hidden Treasures Expedition, and Monty figured he had discovered a pretty big piece of treasure: his Buddy was a Scout! How cool was that?

"One two three," sang Mrs. Tuttle after lunch

as she clapped her hands three times, "eyes on me! Please come and sit criss-cross applesauce in our meeting circle."

Monty sat down cross-legged on the carpet between Lagu Luka and Devin Hightower, wondering if he could somehow get extra credit for his treasure.

"Hi, Waffles," said Devin.

"Hi, Waffles!" echoed Lagu.

Monty pasted a smile on his face. The smile was supposed to say, *Ha-ha, no big deal*. Except the smile was a total lie. He hated being called Waffles. Tristan Thompson-Brown had started it, and now everybody did it. The only person who didn't was Jasmine. Maybe he'd go sit next to her. He started to get up and by mistake stepped on Lagu's hand.

"Ouch!" yelped Lagu.

Monty got off Lagu's hand quick as he could, but by mistake he bumped into Devin on the other side. That should have been no big deal except Devin made a big joke by shouting, "Get off me, Greene!"

and scrambling away, bumping into Emma Robinson. Emma pulled away from Devin and knocked heads with Ella Bakunda. And Emma and Ella both shouted, "Monty, stop!"

"Sorry," said Monty, before he scooted around the circle and plopped down next to Jasmine.

"Monty!" said Mrs. Tuttle. "What do you think you're doing?"

Monty couldn't tell the whole truth—that he was getting away from kids calling him Waffles. He told half the truth. "I wanted to sit somewhere else."

"You mean you picked a spot, and then changed your mind?"

"I guess," said Monty.

"And do you see what happened?"

"I moved?" he asked.

"You hurt your classmates," said Mrs. Tuttle.

Monty thought that was taking it a little far. Yes, he'd stepped on Lagu's hand, and he was sorry for that. But Devin had just been kidding around. And even though Emma and Ella hadn't liked getting bumped into, he didn't think they'd actually gotten hurt.

"Monty, come here, please," said Mrs. Tuttle, and off came decision-aid number one: Monty shouldn't have changed his mind about where he was sitting.

Sometimes Monty couldn't believe grown-ups. How come they blamed you for something that wasn't your fault? He wouldn't have stepped on Lagu's hand in the first place if Lagu and Devin hadn't called him Waffles. And they wouldn't have called him Waffles if Principal Edwards hadn't called him a waffler. And Principal Edwards would never have called him a waffler if Mrs. Tuttle hadn't made Monty go to the office just because he threw a pencil. It was so messed up!

It was so messed up that Monty decided to make an even bigger mess. When Mrs. Tuttle asked if anybody had anything to share about their Buddy, he raised his hand. "I saw my Buddy march in the parade yesterday. And I have three more Buddies," he announced.

Mrs. Tuttle gave him a funny look. "Everyone has one Buddy," she corrected.

"Yeah but I'm, like, really popular," said Monty. "All the kindergartners want to be my Buddy."

The other kids laughed, and Mrs. Tuttle put her hand to her mouth and turned an imaginary key, which meant everybody was supposed to keep their mouths closed with their words inside. Nobody was supposed to talk except her.

"Monty, your Little Buddy is Leo Schwarz. You can't decide to change Buddies. That's not your decision to make."

"I didn't change," he said. "He's still my Buddy. I just added more Buddies."

"Monty," said Mrs. Tuttle. She paused, so he would know that what she was about to say was extra important. "We need cooperators in our classroom. Can you be a cooperator?"

"I am!" said Monty. "This is like being extra cooperative! Because the name of the Expedition is Hidden *Treasures*, not Hidden Treasure, right? So the more Little Buddies I have the more I'm finding Hidden Treasures!"

Jasmine spoke up, "It wasn't really fair, 'cause some of the kids didn't get Big Buddies, and they really wanted one!"

Then Tristan Thompson-Brown said that it wasn't fair for some kids to have more than one Buddy, so he wanted another one, too. Then more kids started talking out of turn. Mrs. Tuttle raised her hand in the air to signal for silence. She didn't get silence, so she rose and walked to her desk and rang her special mallet on her special xylophone.

A chime sounded through the room. *Gong.* A few kids quieted down. She rang it again—*gong*—and a few more kids stopped talking. After the third *gong*, the room was silent. So everybody heard when Mrs. Tuttle asked Monty to come to her desk and plucked off the second Band-Aid for changing his mind about his Kindergarten Buddy. Monty was about to point out that that wasn't fair—he hadn't changed his mind about Leo—when Mrs. Tuttle did something even more unfair. She yanked off the third Band-Aid for changing his mind about being a cooperator.

"That's not fair!" he objected. "You're taking two Band-Aids for the same thing, and it isn't even wrong!"

Mrs. Tuttle shook her head, as if she was truly sad that Monty was such an uncooperative, indecisive kid. "Monty, I do not have time for this. You may go down to the office and tell Mrs. Tracy that you need to speak with the social worker." She pointed to the door.

Monty stepped out of the classroom and into the hallway. Before and after school the hall was jammed with kids and their backpacks, but not now. Now it was empty. It felt strange, being in the hallway all by himself. Walking slowly—because the last thing he wanted to do was talk with the social worker— he passed the fifth graders' yellow lockers and the fourth graders' green lockers and the third graders' orange lockers. At the top of the stairs he stopped by the big window that overlooked the playground.

The rain yesterday had ripped the last leaves from the branches, and all the trees stood bare and brown, like stick figures in a drawing. This is a tree. This is a person. This is a house.

Some kids got to say, "Let's play at my house," and it meant only one thing. They had one house. One home. One family. They didn't know how good they had it! Home used to be the house where Monty lived with his mom and his dad and Sierra. Then there were two different houses. Mom's house and dad's house. There were two different families. The Mom-Bob-Aisha-Sierra family and the Dad-Beth-Audrey-Sierra family. The only thing that stayed the same was Sierra. Who didn't even care about keeping things the same!

"Monty! Hey, wait up!"

It was Lagu, holding a block of wood painted blue—the hallway bathroom pass.

"What do you want?" demanded Monty. "To make fun of me some more?"

"I didn't know!" said Lagu.

"Know what?"

"I didn't know you didn't like Waffles," said Lagu. "I thought it was okay 'cause those guys are your friends."

"That's pretty stupid," said Monty. "How would you like it if I called you Pancake?" he demanded. "Or French Toast?"

Lagu made a serious face, as if he was seriously trying to think about how being called Pancake would make him feel. He held it until suddenly Monty burst out laughing, and then Lagu began laughing, and for a minute they both had a wicked bad fit of the giggles. Then, quickly, before somebody heard and came to investigate, they both pulled it together. They were alone in the hallway, which they shouldn't be. Lagu was supposed to be in the bathroom, and Monty was supposed to be in the office.

Except Monty suddenly decided he wasn't going to the office. He didn't want to find out what happened after the third Band-Aid came off. He wasn't going to talk to the social worker. He had somewhere else to go.

"Hey, Lagu," he said. "Want to do me a favor?"

"Sure!" agreed Lagu. "Like what?"

Monty told Lagu his idea. They would go downstairs. Lagu would go into the office and get Mrs. Tracy's attention so she would have her eye on Lagu, not on the window that overlooked the lobby. Not on Monty, sneaking out.

"You're *leaving*?" asked Lagu, a note of awe in his voice. Kids never left school during the day. Not by themselves.

"I'm leaving," said Monty.

"Wow," said Lagu. "You're going to be in so much trouble!"

"I'm already in trouble," said Monty. "You in?"

Nodding, Lagu whispered, "I'm in."

They tiptoed down the big stairwell to the front lobby, which was empty. Lagu hurried into the office and started waving his arms around, getting Mrs.

Tracy's attention so her back was to the big glass window. *Now!*

Monty pushed against the big, heavy doors, feeling every second as if a troll was going to come rushing out and shout, "You can't cross over my bridge!"

But no shout came.

THE NEXT HOLIDAY IS: THANKSGIVING

Outside, the air felt washed clean after yesterday's rain. The sky was bright blue, as if it had been scrubbed. Monty started walking away. He couldn't believe how easy it was to leave! How come kids didn't walk out all the time? He kept going, past the playground, past the weedy, jungly place between where the playground ended and the houses began, and on down North Street. He was home free!

He wasn't home free.

Or, he was home free for about an hour.

"Monty," said Mrs. Schwarz when she answered his knock on the door. "Is school out already? Down, Noodle!" she said, holding onto the golden retriever's collar so it wouldn't jump on Monty. She had the same golden red hair as the dog. "Come on in. Leo will be so happy to see you."

"Is he sick?"

"Not exactly." Lowering her voice, she started to explain, "We just got some big news this morning, and Leo was kind of upset—" when Leo's voice drowned out his mom's.

"You saw me!" Leo came bounding down the stairs and wrapped his arms around Monty's waist. "You saw me! You saw me! You saw me!"

"I saw you, Scout guy."

"I'm a Lion Cub!"

"Totally," agreed Monty. "I totally saw you being a Lion Cub Scout."

"That was so sweet of you, Monty," said Mrs. Schwarz with a big smile. Still smiling, she looked down at the watch on her wrist. When she looked up again, she wasn't smiling anymore, but all she said was, "Why don't you two play while I make you a snack? Nachos sound good?"

Monty checked out Leo's room and read Leo a

story, and then the nachos were ready. Monty had just put the last cheesy chip in his mouth when there was a knock on the door, and Mrs. Schwarz went to answer it. Monty's hour of freedom was over.

"Thank you so much for calling," said his dad in a grim voice.

"Monty!" said his mom.

And the policewoman got on her radio. "Dispatch? This is twenty-five sixteen. My forty is 267 North Street. I've got the missing boy."

"Monty," said his mom, "what are you *doing* here?"

"I"—began Monty, but couldn't finish his answer because his parents kept lobbing questions at him.

"What made you think you could just walk out of school?" demanded his dad. "Do you know how much trouble you caused?"

"Do you know how worried we were about you?" asked his mom.

The policewoman said, "The law says you need to stay in school."

Monty suddenly recognized her. She was Officer Friendly! She was the one who spoke at school assemblies about things like safety. And graffiti.

"You know what happens to kids who start breaking the law *now*?" asked Officer Friendly. She shook her head, as if she didn't want to describe the path Monty was on—one day you leave school to go see your Reading Buddy, and the next thing you know you're a hardened criminal.

All the answers to all the questions Monty had been asked bounced around in his head. He was here because he couldn't take kids calling him Waffles anymore. Or Mrs. Tuttle ripping Band-Aids off his bare skin.

"I'm on a field trip," he finally said. "There's nothing to worry about and I'm totally safe."

"Well, the field trip is *off*," said Officer Friendly.

"Don't!" shouted Leo, lunging for the policewoman. "Don't yell at him!"

Mrs. Schwarz grabbed Leo and pulled him back, wrapping her arms around him. "I'm sorry, officer," she said.

"It's all right," said the policewoman. She stowed

her radio in a little pocket on her belt and said that since the parents were here and Monty was safe, she would be on her way.

When she had gone Mrs. Schwarz loosened her grip on Leo and turned to Monty's parents. "I just want to say what an incredible kid you have. Leo talks about him all the time, how he has the best Big Buddy of anybody. We don't have any family around here, so it's extra special for Leo to have an older boy to spend time with."

Monty didn't know that. Sometimes he felt like he had too *much* family. But he couldn't imagine not having any family at all. That sounded lonely. Nobody had asked a question, but suddenly Monty got the same feeling as when he had the right answer to a question. He knew what to do next! Because he knew the next holiday!

"Mom—Dad! What house am I at for Thanksgiving this year?" he asked. "Can Leo come?" He worked up his best version of puppy-dog eyes. "Please?"

Monty's mom and dad gave each other a should-we-tell-him-about-that-thing? glance, and his dad gave a quick nod.

"We're doing something a little different this year," said Monty's mom. "We're celebrating together." She turned to Mrs. Schwarz, "And we'd love to have you join us, if you don't have other plans."

Leo barked and tucked his hands under his chin.

"I think that means we'd love to," said Leo's mom.

"Great," said Monty's dad. Then he turned back to Monty. "Which doesn't mean you're not in trouble."

Late that afternoon Monty and his parents went back to Casco Elementary for a meeting with Principal Edwards and Mrs. Tuttle to work out exactly how much trouble he was in. Everybody sat around a table in a little room Monty had never been in before. His feet dangled from the grown-up-size chair, not quite reaching the floor. All the kids had gone home, and the building was quiet. Behind the empty bus circle the sun was the color of an orange Creamsicle.

"I'm very upset," began Monty's mom.

"I understand," said Principal Edwards, "and I am,

too." Her yellow glasses bobbed up and down on the tip of her nose as she nodded, explaining that this had never happened before and she would make sure it never happened again. She had already scheduled an all-staff meeting about safety protocols.

"That's not what I meant," said Monty's mom. "Yes—we're all upset that Monty was able to walk out of school. But what I'm really upset about is *why* he wanted to walk out. Those Band-Aids."

Monty's dad chimed in. "Those are kind of over-the-top," he agreed. "I'm not saying there's not a problem with Monty making up his mind. But it seems like the Band-Aids aren't much of a solution."

Monty's mom was sticking up for him—no surprise—she'd wanted to talk to Mrs. Tuttle from the first minute she knew about the decision-aids. But—big surprise—so was his dad! Now, what would the principal say?

Principal Edwards took off her yellow glasses and polished the lenses with a tissue, then mounted them on her nose again. "I agree," she said. "That strategy hasn't been effective. I think we should discontinue the decision-aids. What do you think, Mrs. Tuttle?"

Monty held his breath, waiting to hear what his teacher would say. Behind her, through the window, he could see the Creamsicle sun melting, turning the whole sky orange.

Mrs. Tuttle swept her long black hair over her shoulder. "I agree, too."

Monty was so surprised he hardly listened to what his parents and the principal were saying now, but he could hear the cheerful notes of their voices.

Monty knew better than to feel cheerful. He knew that Mrs. Tuttle had just gone along because the principal was making her. And that even if his teacher was smiling and nodding now, during the meeting, she wasn't going to give up that easily. She might have to stop sticking actual Band-Aids on him, but there was no way she wouldn't stick to her goal. It was only November. If it took Mrs. Tuttle all year, she was going to turn Monty into a mind-maker-upper.

THANKSGIVING DAY

Sometimes Monty couldn't figure grown-ups out. Mostly he couldn't. Before, he and Sierra had Thanksgiving with their mom one year, and the next year with their dad. Now with this flip-flop business they were splitting up him and Sierra most of the time, but teaming up on the holiday. Which felt totally unfair—the first time his parents decide to do Thanksgiving together in an extra-huge party is the first time him and Sierra are at different houses, but *he's* at the house where the dinner is so *he's* the one who has to do all the work! Clear all the shoes out of the front hall. Polish the silver candlesticks. Go snip some parsley from the garden. Answer the door.

"Monty!" called his mom. "There's the bell! Answer the door!"

Monty ran to the door. First came Sierra, looking unhappy in a dress and tights and shoes that weren't sneakers.

"Dad made me dress up," she whispered. *"To show respect,"* she mimicked, in her imitation-dad voice.

"Well, Mom made me do all the work!" said Monty. He repeated his mom's instructions in his imitation-mom voice. *"Do this! Do that! And do it cheerfully!"*

Sierra grinned. "How's Little A?"

Monty grinned back. "Noisy," he said. "How's Big A?"

"Bossy," said Sierra.

"Stop talking about me," ordered Audrey, coming up the steps in boots so puffy it looked as if each one was a tiny sheep attached to her foot. Her blond hair crisscrossed her head in fancy braids. "I know you're talking about me."

"We are not," lied Monty.

"Honest," agreed Sierra. "We're not."

"Whatever," said Audrey. "Like I care."

Behind Sierra came Beth, wearing a bright gold and orange scarf and carrying a pie, and behind Beth came Mr. Sherman, Audrey's dad, who had been invited so he wouldn't have to be alone on Thanksgiving. And behind them came Mrs. Schwarz with Harriet and Leo. Leo was wearing his khaki-colored Lion Cub shirt and a miniature navy blue necktie.

When everyone was seated at the table, Leo tugged Monty's sleeve. "Who are all these people?"

Explaining Monty's family was complicated. Maybe they should be wearing name tags, like when somebody visited his class and Mrs. Tuttle made them write their names on stickers. But even that wouldn't explain exactly who they were. He should have made one of those programs you got when you went to see a show, with a list of the cast of characters.

Monty Greene. That was him.

Sierra Greene, his twin sister.

Their mom, Helen Greene-Day.

Their stepdad, Bob Day.

Aisha Day, Mom and Bob's new baby.

Monty and Sierra's dad, John Greene.

Their stepmom, Beth Sherman-Greene.

Beth's daughter, Audrey Sherman.

And Mr. Sherman, Audrey's dad.

Since Monty hadn't printed up a program with the cast of characters, maybe he should introduce them. Or maybe not. Maybe everybody could introduce themselves. Monty did something he had seen grown-ups do. He tapped his knife on his water glass. *Ding! Ding! Ding!*

"Hey, everybody!" he said. "Announcement! I have a favor to ask. Can we all go around and say our names? For Leo?"

Monty's mom was spooning applesauce into Aisha. "Good idea," she said. "Who'll go first?"

"I will," said Audrey's dad, rising. He wore a pair of tiny, rimless glasses, and a big, bushy beard. "My name is Edward Sherman, and I would like to give thanks to all of you for including me in your celebration, so I can be with my daughter, Audrey." He turned to Audrey, sitting beside him. "Your turn!"

"I'm Audrey Sherman," mumbled Audrey.

Audrey's dad told her to stand up and speak up. Audrey's mom added, "And that was nice, Edward, that you said what you were thankful for. Can we all do that, since it is Thanksgiving?"

Standing, Audrey gave Monty a cold stare that meant he was going to pay for this later. "I'm Audrey Sherman!" she shouted. "And I'm thankful for . . . turkey! Yeah: I'm thankful for turkey."

Audrey's mom was next to Audrey so she stood next. "My name is Beth Sherman-Greene. I want to give thanks to Helen and Bob for inviting us."

This was out of control! Monty had figured people could say their names so he wouldn't have to, and now everybody was standing up and giving thanks! What was he supposed to say when it was his turn?

His stepdad rose from his seat. Bob never dressed

up, so as usual, he was wearing a T-shirt with a message: BE YOURSELF. EVERYONE ELSE IS ALREADY TAKEN. He wanted to give thanks to the next generation—Audrey and Sierra and Monty and Aisha. And Harriet and Leo, too.

Aisha was in a high chair in between Bob and Monty's mom; she was too young to go. She just said, "Buh!" and everybody laughed. Maybe Monty could try saying "Buh!"

Next Monty's mom gave thanks for having enough to eat, and all the delicious foods, especially brussels sprouts, which she loved, and the pumpkin pie Beth had brought. Monty didn't know which was sillier—giving thanks to children or vegetables. He did know that he had no idea what he was going to say.

The introductions and the eating kept going. Platters of food were passed around the table. Turkey. Gravy. Mashed potatoes. Cranberry sauce. The brussels sprouts went by, which Monty was definitely *not* thankful for, because they stank. He was stuffing himself with more stuffing when Sierra stood up.

"I'm Sierra Greene," she announced. "And I'm thankful because I scored a goal in my last game."

"Does that count?" demanded Audrey. "Isn't that more like bragging than giving thanks?"

Audrey's mom and dad scolded her in unison: "Audrey!"

Big A couldn't talk about Sierra like that! "It's better than *turkey!*" blurted Monty.

Now it was the turn of Monty's mom and dad to scold *him* in unison. "Monty!"

Sierra sat down and put a heaping spoonful of cranberry sauce straight in her mouth, and Monty's dad pushed back his chair and stood up. He looked like some kind of alternate universe dad, with his familiar going-bald-pronto shaved head, but wearing a dress-up shirt and tie instead of his usual paint-splattered plaid shirt.

"I'm John Greene, and I'm thankful for new friends," he said, raising his glass in the direction of the Schwarz family—Mrs. Schwarz, Harriet, and Leo. "And new Scouts!" he added, his voice tripping, as if his tie was so tight it was choking him.

Monty wondered if his dad was thinking about his own dad again, who had gone all the way to Eagle Scout. His dad sat down, and Sierra reached over and patted his smooth head. "Good effort, Dad," she said.

Soon it would be Monty's turn. Seriously, what was he thankful for? He liked the stuffing and the mashed potatoes and the gravy, but he didn't want to say a food. It should be something more important than that. He was thankful that Mrs. Tuttle wasn't putting Band-Aids on his arm and ripping them off anymore. But no way was he going to thank Mrs. Tuttle just because his mom made her stop being so mean. Should he thank his mom? But the decision to stop the decision-aids happened at the special conference, which wouldn't have happened at all unless he'd walked out of school, which he wouldn't have done unless he wanted to go see Leo. So maybe Monty should thank Leo.

As Leo's mom stood for her turn, Monty took

another bite of stuffing. Trying to think about where thankfulness for something began made Monty feel as if he was riding in a car speeding in reverse. You could go further and further back in time. It was like when he went to the parade with his dad, and thought about the time before he was born. Before Monty was born, there was a time when his dad hadn't even known Monty's mom, and even before that, a time when his dad was a kid himself.

"Wow!" said his mom. "New Jersey! That's big news!"

What? What was big news? Something about New Jersey? Monty had been spacing out. Now he tuned back in.

"Why New Jersey?" asked Monty's dad.

"That's where my whole family lives, and Leo's dad, too," said Mrs. Schwarz. "I've been thinking about it for a while, and now I've got a job offer." She drew a big breath, as if she needed more air to keep talking. "So we're going to move." She was going on and on, talking about *transitions* and *opportunities*, and how good it would be for Leo and Harriet to be closer to their dad. Finally she trailed off, and for a second nobody said anything.

"Yeah, but *when*?" blurted Monty.

Yesterday Mrs. Tuttle had announced the date for their Culminating Event: next Wednesday, December 3. They would be serving a special brunch in the cafetorium (she needed all students to ask their mom or dad for a food contribution) and the school band would be performing.

"This weekend, actually," explained Leo's mom.

"But what about the Culminating Event?" burst out Monty. "You'll miss it!"

Audrey's dad asked, "What's a Culminating Event?"

Audrey sighed loudly. "It's what they do at the end of a Learning Expedition, Dad. To show everybody how much you learned."

Leo's sister, Harriet, who had been at Casco Elementary last year, spoke up. "It's a really big deal. You have a party, and everybody shows the work they did."

"There's gonna be food," said Monty, "and the band is learning songs!"

"Do you play in the band?" asked Audrey's dad, Mr. Sherman.

"Flute!" snickered Audrey, lifting her hands and wiggling her fingers, as if she was playing an imaginary flute. "La la la, I play the flute."

Monty wanted to tell Audrey to shut *up*, but he managed to keep his mouth shut. He had bigger problems than Audrey.

"Leo has to be there," he explained. "He's my Little Buddy!"

"I told you!" cried Leo to his mom.

Harriet added, "I told you, Mom."

Nodding, Leo's mom said, "I know you did." To the whole group she explained that she had planned on moving after the New Year, but her new boss needed her to start as soon as possible, and she needed the job too much to say no. She wished she could make things turn out differently, but she couldn't. And she hoped— for Leo's sake—that Monty would understand.

Monty could feel everybody staring at him, waiting to see if he would understand. He understood perfectly! He was supposed to act like everything was okay in front of Leo. Even though it wasn't! Grown-ups claimed they wanted you to tell the truth, but they didn't! If he actually told the truth about how he really felt, he'd be in big-time trouble.

"It's okay," he lied. "It's not that big a deal."

Sierra piped up, "It *is too* a big deal," earning herself the next parental scolding.

"*Sierra,*" shushed their mom and dad in unison.

"I'm just *saying*," insisted Sierra, "the Culminating Event is a really big deal."

"Well you can just *not say* anything else right now," scolded their mom.

There was an awkward silence, broken by Monty's stepdad asking who wanted seconds on turkey, and his stepmom saying she did. The round of introductions had been interrupted, and never got started again. If Monty had gotten a turn, he knew what he'd say he was thankful for now. Sierra. Telling the truth. Sticking up for him.

The rest of the meal went by in a blur. Platters were passed around one last time. Desert was served. Aisha got put in her crib for a nap, and Monty asked if he and Leo could be excused. Upstairs, Monty scooped the rat from its cage and plunked it on Leo's shoulder.

"Name?" asked Leo.

"Samuel Whiskers," said Monty. "I think."

"That tickles, Samuel Whiskers!" said Leo, giggling, as the rat scrambled over to his other shoulder. He sat down on the bed and looked up at Monty. "I'm moving to New Jersey," he said.

Monty didn't know what to say. The rat was traveling back and forth across the back of Leo's neck, as if it couldn't decide where to be. Monty thought of stories where a tiny angel perches on somebody's shoulder, trying to get them to be good, and a tiny devil perches on the other shoulder, telling them to be bad. And the person has to decide which voice to listen to.

The angel-rat would say, *Don't make a fuss about Leo moving away. Pretend it's no big deal. For Leo's sake. Tell him how it'll be great because he can see his dad all the time now.* The devil-rat would say, *Why should you have to make believe everything's fine when it's not?*

No, that wasn't right. The rat clambered back and forth on Leo, and Monty went back and forth in his head, trying to figure out which voice to listen to.

"Leo!" came the voice of Leo's mom up the stairs. "Five minutes!"

Monty felt lame. He couldn't decide what to say to Leo. He couldn't even decide on a name for his rat. He couldn't decide anything. Maybe he really was a waffler.

"Leo!" called Leo's mom again, and Monty's mom called, "Monty!" Which was when Leo started yelling, "I don't want to go!"

Monty didn't know if Leo meant he didn't want to go home right now, or he didn't want to go to New Jersey. Maybe both. But whatever Leo meant, he yelled it so loud that the rat freaked, because when Monty reached for the rat it just held on more tightly. Gently, he tried to pry the rat away, but the rat kept clinging to Leo.

Monty's dad's voice boomed up the stairwell. "Monty! Did you hear?"

"I heard!" shouted Monty. "We're coming!"

"I don't want to go!" wailed Leo.

Great, thought Monty. He had a freaked-out kid and a freaked-out rat. He needed to get the rat off Leo and get Leo downstairs. "How about I walk you home?" he asked. "Sound good?"

Leo sniffed but didn't scream. Thinking about it.

"And we'll ask your mom if you can come over tomorrow, okay?"

Leo sniffed again. "Okay," he finally said.

"Monty," barked his dad. "Downstairs, pronto!"

"We're coming," shouted Monty, and with one final tug he plucked the rat from Leo's shoulder, lowered him into the cage, set the lid on top, and hurried downstairs.

GIVING THANKS FOR REAL

"**Of course I** put the cover on!" shouted Monty. "I always do!"

Monty was sure he'd put the cover on the rat's cage. He tried to think back. He'd been hanging out with Leo and the rat when it was time for Leo to go home. He had put the rat *in* the cage and the cover *on* the cage and then . . . had he put the dictionaries on top of the cover to weigh it down? He was sure he had. He always did. Except there were the dictionaries on his bureau. And the rat was gone. They were like little Houdinis, the guy at the pet store had said. They loved to escape.

"I'm sorry I asked that," said his mom wearily. "Of course you did, and besides, it doesn't really matter now. But we've looked everywhere, and it's ten o'clock, and it's time for bed. We can keep looking in the morning."

"He'll probably turn up," said Bob.

"He's not like a toy!" shouted Monty. "He's not going to *turn up*. If he turns up, he'll probably be dead! We have to find him!"

One more time, they searched the house. Upstairs: Monty's room, Aisha and Sierra's room (Aisha sleeping, Sierra's bed empty), his mom and Bob's room. Downstairs: kitchen (still smelling like Thanksgiving dinner), dining room (the table still extra-big, covered with a white cloth), living room. He even opened the door to the room where his mom worked, and flicked on the light. The little skeleton spooked him. It was a miniature replica of a real skeleton that his mom had gotten to learn all the bones of the body. She'd kept it to teach people about what was inside them—what was hurting them, and why. With the skeleton dangling in the corner, Monty looked for the rat as quickly as he could, turned off the light, and closed the door.

"Monty, go to bed," said his mom. "We'll keep looking in the morning."

"Promise you'll wake me if you find him, okay?" demanded Monty.

"Promise," said his mom.

Monty didn't know how many hours later it was when his mom woke him. She was sitting on the edge of his bed. The room was dark, except for a thin beam of light shining in from the hallway, and the house was so quiet that he heard the warning sound of the foghorn way out on the ocean. In the dark quiet his mom whispered, "Monty."

He could tell from the sound of her voice that the rat was dead.

Suddenly Monty felt wide awake. "I told you so!" he accused her. "I *told* you he wouldn't just turn up. I *told* you he'd be dead."

"I'm so sorry, Monty," she said. She reached to hug him, but he pulled away.

Sorry was a funny word. Sometimes it meant a person was apologizing for hurting you. That made sense. But sometimes it meant they were sad that you'd gotten hurt, even though it wasn't their fault. For some reason, that kind of *sorry* made Monty mad. What good did it do? Just saying they were sorry didn't help!

"It's not your fault!" he said angrily.

"Not that kind of sorry," she said. "I mean . . . I'm just sorry it happened."

"Where is he?"

"Downstairs."

Monty pushed away the covers, got out of bed, and followed his mom down the stairs and into the kitchen. She turned on the light, pointed to a towel in a laundry basket on the floor.

"I was up nursing Aisha," she said, "and then afterward I came downstairs for a snack. The bathroom light was on so I went in to shut it off, and that's when I saw the rat. I don't know if he was trying to get a drink, or what, but I guess he climbed into the . . . um . . . toilet, and drowned."

Monty crouched down on the floor. He reached

into the basket and pulled back the towel. There was his rat. Stiff and wet and freezing cold. Dead. He started to cry. He *hated* crying! His mom tried to hug him, but he pulled away. He didn't want to feel better. His rat was dead, and it was his fault.

When Monty woke up the next morning he lay in bed for a long time, because what was the point of getting up? Just like last night, he heard the moaning note of the foghorn. Then he heard the ding-dong note of the doorbell, and his mom called up the stairs that Leo was here.

Leo? Oh, no: Leo. Monty had forgotten all about inviting Leo over today. He hauled himself out of bed and went downstairs to the kitchen. There was a big pot of turkey bones simmering on the stove, and the laundry basket with the bundled-up towel on the floor. There was his mom, chopping vegetables, and Aisha in her bouncy seat. And there was Leo, who didn't waste any time.

"Can I hold Samuel Whiskers?"

Monty didn't know the right way to tell Leo, so he blurted out all at once, "He got out of his cage—and fell into the toilet—and drowned."

"Drowned?"

Nodding, Monty pointed to the basket. "Drowned. Like, dead."

Leo crumpled to the floor, like when all the air came out of a balloon. Monty plunked himself down beside him. Together they sat beside the basket. Finally Leo offered, "My grandpa died."

"Mine, too," said Monty.

"Are you gonna bury him?"

"I don't know," said Monty. "I guess."

"My grandpa got buried. They put his name on a stone." Leo pointed to the basket. "Are you gonna put his name on a stone?"

"I guess," repeated Monty. "Except—I don't know."

"Don't know what?"

Monty felt bad all over again. He had tried a few names for the rat, but never settled on one. And now the rat was dead, without a real name. Because he was a waffler. "I don't know his name, for sure."

Leo started listing all the names. "There was Mack."

"Short for McIntosh," agreed Monty.

"And Officer Rat," remembered Leo.

Monty went down the list. "Scratcher," he said.

"And Samuel Whiskers," finished Leo. Giggling, he jumbled the names together: "Officer Samuel Scratcher McIntosh Whiskers."

Monty grinned. Who cared if he couldn't decide on a name? Leo didn't! "I like it," he said. "Officer Samuel Scratcher McIntosh Whiskers."

"The third!" said Leo.

"Officer Samuel Scratcher McIntosh Whiskers the third," agreed Monty. "Mack for short." Monty felt better. He wanted to do something nice for Leo. "So, New Jersey," he said. "That's where your dad lives, right? Leonard Schwarz Junior?"

Leo nodded glumly. "I'll miss the party."

"The band is terrible," said Monty, shrugging. "I'll probably quit soon."

"How come?"

Monty hesitated. His mom was right there, chopping vegetables. But who cared if she heard? "I don't like the flute."

Leo nodded, as if he understood. "Flute's stupid," he said loyally.

"I want to play the trumpet," added Monty.

"Trumpet's awesome!" said Leo.

Monty smiled. He was going to miss this kid. He pointed to the basket. "You want to see him one last time?"

Leo nodded yes.

Reaching into the basket, Monty put his hand on the towel, but then snatched it right back, screaming, "Aaah!"

Leo cried, "What, what, what?" and Aisha answered his scream with one of her own, and Monty's mom put down the carrot she was chopping and picked up the baby.

"Monty, what is it?"

"I felt something move," said Monty.

Something was moving inside him, too. Fear and hope pushing at each other. Reaching over, he pulled open the towel.

The rat looked up at him. Eyes open. Whiskers wriggling.

"*Whoa!*" said Monty. "He's not dead! *Whoa!*" he repeated.

"*Whoa,*" echoed Leo.

Holding Aisha, Monty's mom peered down at the rat. "I've always heard rats could survive almost anything, and I guess it's true. He must have just seemed dead last night because he was so cold, and then he warmed up in the towel and he was okay! Do you think?"

What Leo must have thought was that he liked the sound of the word *whoa.* "*Whoa,*" he said again. And again. "*Whoa.*"

What Monty thought was that this was the right time to take the turn he had missed yesterday. He stood up. "My name is Monty Greene," he announced, "and I'm thankful that my rat—Officer Samuel Scratcher McIntosh Whiskers the third—is still alive."

ONE BUDDY OR NOBODY

"**M**onty," said **Mrs.** Tuttle on Monday morning. "Come here, please."

Monty walked slowly over to his teacher's desk, the way he used to when he still had to get the day's decision-aids put on. She might have stopped putting Band-Aids on him and ripping them off, but she was still a little scary, with her list of expectations as long as her long, black hair.

"Monty, Mrs. Calhoun has told me that Leo won't be in school anymore."

"I know," said Monty. "He's moving to New Jersey."

The rest of the fourth grade was gathering around Mrs. Tuttle's desk, listening: Jasmine Raines, the Town Crier, with about a hundred rainbow clips in her hair; Lagu Luka, who didn't call Monty Waffles anymore, and orange-haired Tristan Thompson-Brown, who did, but who never got in trouble; Devin Hightower, with his glasses strapped around his head; Emma Robinson and Ella Bakunda, Monty's fellow flute players; Ethan Ho and the other kids.

"Mrs. Calhoun and I have talked this over," said Mrs. Tuttle, "and we have an idea." She sounded hopeful.

Mrs. Tuttle's hopeful voice did not make Monty feel full of hope. Her last big idea for Monty had been the decision-aids.

"Due to this unusual situation," she said, "we've decided to let you partner with one of the kinder-gartners who didn't get a Buddy." She beamed at Monty, as if she'd just given him a wonderful gift and couldn't wait to hear his reaction.

It seemed like Mrs. Tuttle was actually trying to be nice. So how come she couldn't see why picking a new Buddy was the opposite of nice? Which kid would he pick? Kieran from the nut-free table?

Lagu's little sister, Winnie? Or Finn? They *all* felt like his Little Buddy.

"But I told you, I have three extra Buddies! I can't ask just one of them!"

"Of course not," said Mrs. Tuttle, nodding. "We wouldn't ask *you* to make that decision. We're just offering you the chance to have a new Buddy. Mrs. Calhoun and I can decide who that will be."

"But you can't do that!" he protested. "You can't pick just one! That would still leave two kids out!"

"That could hurt somebody's *feelings!*" cried Jasmine, and Emma Robinson and Ella Bakunda agreed that hurting feelings was *wrong*. Everybody knew that.

Mrs. Tuttle's beaming smile was gone. Wearing the same I'm-being-patient look on her face that Monty's dad sometimes did, she launched into a long explanation of how nobody was being left out. The Hidden Treasures Culminating Event was to show all parents of students in Mrs. Calhoun's kindergarten and Mrs. Tuttle's fourth grade what they had learned this fall. Reading Buddies would show the books they had read together, and the other kindergartners would simply show what they had been working on in their special services. So Monty didn't need to worry. Everyone would be at the Culminating Event. Nobody would be left out. All he needed to do was say if he wanted to accept Mrs. Calhoun's offer to let him partner with one of her students.

Monty thought about the offer. Leo was gone. Monty could say yes to a new Buddy. But saying yes meant that one little kid was going to be happy and two little kids were going to be totally bummed. That wasn't fair! Monty didn't want to say yes, but he didn't want to say no, either.

"Why can't they all be my Buddy?"

By now Mrs. Tuttle's patient face was gone, too. "Because," she said, "everybody else has one. People don't get everything they want just because they can't make up their mind! You can make up your mind to have one Buddy"—she picked up her special mallet—"or no Buddy." She tapped the mallet on the xylophone, and a note rang through the room: this conversation was over.

Mrs. Tuttle's words stuck in his head, like a song. *One Buddy or no Buddy. One Buddy or no Buddy.* Then he thought how "no Buddy" sounded like "nobody," so Monty added that to the song. *One Buddy or no Buddy, and no Buddy means nobody.*

Monty still had the song stuck in his head when it was time for band.

"Good morning, musicians!" cried Mr. Carlson, the band teacher. He always started off super cheerfully, but by the end of the period he always looked as if he had a headache. Today he was wearing a white shirt and a red tie dotted with tiny musical notes.

He made the official band teacher signal for silence, tapping his baton against his music stand. "Does everybody see what I am wearing?" he asked, and answered his own question. "I am wearing dress clothes! Why? To show you appropriate concert attire! Our performance for the Hidden Treasures

Culminating Event is the *day after tomorrow*! So, musicians, please take out your sheet music for 'Merrily We Roll Along.'"

Mr. Carlson held his baton aloft, the signal for them to get their instruments into playing position. Monty put his flute to his mouth, and on either side of him, Ella Bakunda and Emma Robinson picked up their flutes. There weren't enough music stands to go around, so the two girls shared with him.

When they started playing "Merrily We Roll Along," Monty still couldn't get the ditty out of his head: *one Buddy or no Buddy, and no Buddy means nobody*. After a few bars, Mr. Carlson shouted, "Flutes! *Flutes!*"

Most grown-ups used your whole name when you were in trouble. Mr. Carlson was different. If he was happy with you, he used your real name: Monty Greene. If he called you by the name of your instrument, he was *not* happy.

"Flutes!" he roared again.

Monty and Ella and Emma put their flutes in their laps and looked up at Mr. Carlson, his hand in a tight fist around his baton.

"I am conducting 'Merrily We Roll Along'! Is that what you are playing?"

That was one of those questions they weren't really supposed to answer, because it wasn't the real question. What Mr. Carlson really meant was: why do you flutes sound so awful?

Monty knew the answer. The flutes weren't all awful. *He* was, because his brain was singing the *Nobody* song stuck in his head. He started to say, "Sorry," when Emma Robinson interrupted.

"We had the wrong music," she said, which wasn't true. "Sorry, Mr. C."

Ella Bakunda joined in the not-truth. She grabbed the sheet music and pretended to stuff it in her music folder, then took the same sheet back out again and put it on the stand, as if she had the correct song now.

"'Merrily We Roll Along,'" she said. "Right?"

"That is right," said Mr. Carlson wearily. "Thank you, Miss Bakunda." He tapped his baton again, and in a voice halfway between beginning-of-the-class cheerful and end-of-the-class headache, cried, "Let's take it from the top!"

At recess the *No Buddy means nobody, no Buddy means nobody* song was still running in circles around his brain as Monty ran to his usual spot at the edge of the field, and tagged the chain-link fence. On the other side of the fence the bare branches of the sumac trees stuck up into the blue sky at crazy angles. The branches made Monty think of the little skeleton hanging in his mom's workroom. Bones were hidden inside a body, like tree branches hidden underneath leaves in the summer. It'd be weird if you could see the bones inside somebody, the same way you saw tree branches in the wintertime.

It was weird that some people could already see inside him sometimes. Like Sierra, who knew that the Culminating Event was a big deal, and who had stuck up for him at Thanksgiving dinner, even though it meant she got scolded. And who was now making a beeline across the playground in her red high-tops, trailed by a pack of girls. She was breathing hard from running when she reached him.

"What are you going to do now?" she demanded.

"About what?"

"The Culminating Event!" she said.

Jasmine was right behind his sister. "I told her what Mrs. Tuttle said," she announced, with a proud look on her face, as if she'd done a good deed. "About how you could get a new Buddy, but you said you have three Buddies!"

Sierra grinned at Monty. She didn't have to say the words out loud for Monty to know what she was thinking: *what did you expect from the Town Crier?* Monty grinned back: *no kidding.* Of course Jasmine had told Sierra. He didn't even care. Because what difference did it make? Mrs. Tuttle wasn't going to budge.

Ella and Emma spoke next.

"Hey, you owe me," Emma pointed out.

"Me, too," echoed Ella. "We covered for you in Band."

"I know," said Monty, bouncing lightly against the chain-link fence. "How come?"

Ella shrugged. "'Cause it's not fair."

Monty nodded. In a way, it didn't make sense. Mr. Carlson didn't have anything to do with Mrs. Tuttle's one-Buddy rule. But in another way it made perfect sense. Teachers were on the same team, and kids were on the same team. Emma and Ella were on his side, and that meant covering for Monty when he messed up in Band.

"Thanks," said Monty. "I owe you guys."

"We know that," said Ella.

"So what are you going to do?" asked Emma.

"I don't know!" said Monty.

How come people expected him to *do* something, anyway? Overhead, a bunch of crows were zigging and zagging across the blue sky, and on the playground, more kids were racing toward Monty's spot by the chain-link fence. Monty was glad to see Lagu heading over. He only felt medium-glad about Devin Hightower. Devin didn't call him Waffles all the time, more like whenever he seemed to remember. Which was usually whenever Tristan Thompson-Brown was around. Which was why Monty wasn't at all glad to see Tristan arrive.

"Hey, Waffles!" said Tristan. He was wearing a winter hat so you couldn't see his bright orange not-me hair. "How come you're not babysitting today?"

"They're not babies," said Monty.

"They're mini-waffles!" cried Tristan. "Get it? Waffles and his mini-waffles?"

Monty bounced harder against the chain-link fence. So what if he had a few friends in kindergarten? At least they never called him Waffles. Half of Monty wanted to tell Tristan off, but half of him didn't dare. The two halves started having a fight inside his head.

Tell him to quit it.

No way. Then he'll know it bothers you.

Way. Otherwise he'll never stop.

He never will stop.

Make him.

How?

Monty kept bouncing against the chain-link fence. Tristan was calling him a name about not being able to make up his mind, and he couldn't even make up his mind to tell him off! Monty was going through the argument with himself again, when the worst possible thing happened.

Sierra stepped forward. Planting her red sneakers in the grass, his sister said, "Quit it, Tristan."

"What?" asked Tristan.

"Quit calling Monty Waffles."

"Why?"

"He doesn't like it," said Sierra.

"He doesn't care," said Tristan. "It's just a joke. Right, Waffles?"

Everyone was waiting to hear Monty's answer. Sierra and Jasmine. Ella and Emma. Devin and Lagu. Monty was waiting, too. What should he say? He felt his heart doing the alarm clock pound. *Hurry up, hurry up!* Then, like a real alarm clock, the bell rang to mark the end of recess, and all the kids lit off across the playground to get in line for lunch. *Too late! Too late!* He hadn't made up his mind what to say to Tristan. And now Tristan would never stop calling him Waffles. Because that's what he was. A waffler.

REFUSE TO CHOOSE

"**S**o, my friend," said Mr. Milkovich as the bus pulled out of the bus circle, "not such a good day?"

Great, thought Monty. Apparently Mr. Milkovich was another one of those people who had X-ray vision when it came to seeing inside him.

"Not really," he admitted, staring out the bus window as the bus glided along. Across the road, the hill sloped down to where the gray ocean looked up at the gray sky. In a little while, Mr. Milkovich began slowing for the first stop. The stop signs came out from the sides of the bus, like wings, and the red flashers flashed. Traffic slowed, then stopped. From the back of the bus trooped some fifth-grade guys.

"Bye, Waffles."

"Bye, Waffles."

"Bye, Waffles," said the last one. "Bye, Mr. Milk."

Glancing at Monty in the mirror, Mr. Milkovich pulled the door shut and made the stop signs fold back against the bus. Monty felt as if *he* had X-ray vision now. He could tell from the look on the bus driver's face what he was thinking: *That's one of your problems, right? The nickname?* But Mr. Milkovich was too smart to say it out loud. He knew that would just make more trouble for Monty. Unlike Sierra.

"I got same problem," said Mr. Milkovich.

"Really?" asked Monty, suddenly realizing how dense he had been. Maybe Mr. Milkovich didn't like being called Mr. Milk for short!

"But it's only for sometimes," said the driver with a shrug. "You know, sometimes it's problem, sometimes no problem."

At the next stop Kieran, the littlest nut-free sister, came up the aisle and sang out, "Bye, Mr. Milk!"

"Bye-bye!" said Mr. Milkovich to the little girl.

"See you tomorrow!" To Monty he explained, "You see, it's for sometimes no problem?"

Monty got it. Kieran wasn't trying to be mean. The fifth grader was. Just like Tristan. But how come Tristan was trying to be mean? Monty hadn't done anything to him!

Behind Kieran came her sisters, Kelsey and Katy, and Sierra, who was friends with Katy. The nut-free sisters got off the bus and Sierra sat down beside Monty. "Hey," she said, heaving a big sigh. "What house am I at today?"

"Dad's," answered Monty. "I'm at Mom's." Then he blurted, "Why did you say that to Tristan?"

"I was just trying to help!" she said.

"That's like the *opposite* of help," argued Monty. "He's never going to drop it now!"

"I just thought—it just makes me—" she began, then stopped and bit her lip, as if she was thinking. "I guess that was kind of stupid."

"Totally," agreed Monty. "That was totally stupid."

Sierra didn't argue about being stupid, which made Monty a tiny bit less mad. "So what are you going to do?" she asked. "Are you going to get a new Buddy?"

"How can I?" asked Monty. "They all think I'm their Buddy!"

He and Sierra were still talking about Mrs. Tuttle and the Buddy problem when the bus slowed down for Monty's stop. Which was how he and Sierra got off at the same stop for the first time in—Monty didn't know in how long. September and October, Sierra hadn't ridden the bus because she'd gone straight to soccer practice after school. And ever since the Veterans Day parade in November, they'd been flip-flopping houses.

It felt strange, going home together, for the first time in a long time. And in another way, it felt the opposite of strange, because they'd been going home together for years. Side by side, they walked along the brick sidewalk until they got to their mom's. They walked past the sunflowers standing guard by the back door—by now squirrels had taken all the seeds—and went inside. Monty grabbed an apple and headed upstairs, with Sierra still following.

He took the rat from its cage. "Want to hold him?"

"Sure," said Sierra.

She sat down on a beanbag chair and Monty put the rat in her hands.

"Want to feed him?"

Sierra nodded, and Monty showed her how he bit off little nibbles of apple and fed them to the rat. Then he pulled a big bag from his top drawer and dumped the contents on his bed. His sister gasped when she saw the stash.

"You still have Halloween candy?"

"Just some." He'd eaten all his favorites but still had some not-favorites left.

"Sweet!" she said, looking longingly at the leftovers—gummy worms, sour balls, and butterscotches.

"Go ahead," he said.

He took his rat from his sister and perched him on his shoulder, and Sierra took a piece of licorice and settled back on the beanbag.

"So," she asked, nibbling away at the red rope of candy, "what's his name now?"

Monty put a gummy worm in his mouth. Then he put in a sour ball. Which was kind of gross. But kind of good, too. "Officer Samuel Scratcher McIntosh Whiskers the third," he answered, his mouth full of sweet and sour together.

"Officer Samuel Scratcher McIntosh Whiskers the third?" repeated Sierra, laughing. "You just gave him every name, because you couldn't choose one? Good one!"

"Yeah, it is," boasted Monty, agreeing.

Because Sierra hadn't said *good one* in a mean way. She had said it in a nice way, like Kieran calling Mr. Milkovich Mr. Milk was nice, not mean. This was how after school was supposed to be. The rat balancing on his shoulder, hanging out. Sierra hanging out, eating candy.

She finished her licorice and studied the last few pieces of candy on the bedspread.

"Here," said Monty. He took one more piece for

himself, scooped up the rest and dropped it into her hand. "You don't have to choose," he said as he popped the last candy into his mouth.

Sour lime burst onto his tongue and an idea burst into his brain. The Kieran-Winnie-Finn idea. "I'm not going to."

Sierra unwrapped the cellophane from a butterscotch. "What are you talking about?" she asked. "The candy, or a name for your rat?"

"Neither," he explained. "I'm talking about my Buddies. I'm not going to choose one. I refuse."

Sierra giggled. "You refuse to choose?"

"I refuse to choose," he agreed.

"So you're not going to be anybody's Buddy?"

"No," said Monty, shaking his head. "I'm going to be everybody's."

Monty could hardly wait for recess on Tuesday, to tell them. But halfway through the next morning, Jasmine Raines gave a shout. "It's snowing!"

Mrs. Tuttle didn't even try and stop everybody

from running to the windows to watch the first snow of the year. Huge flakes were fluttering down from the sky. In five minutes a sprinkling of snow lay on the playground, like powdered sugar on a pancake. In fifteen minutes the snow was so thick it looked as if a whole box of sugar had been dumped on the pancake. And half an hour later Mrs. Tracy's voice came over the intercom.

"Due to the snow, we will have indoor recess today. Please dress for outdoor weather tomorrow. That means mittens!"

Indoor recess? How was he supposed to tell Kieran, Winnie, and Finn about being his official Buddies at the Culminating Event tomorrow if they were all stuck inside during recess today? He was looking around the room, trying to plot his escape, when Mrs. Tuttle dashed any hope of that.

"Monty," she said. "I hope you're going to make a good choice for indoor recess."

"I am," he said.

"What are you going to do?"

"Could I go to the library?" he tried.

"No," said Mrs. Tuttle, shaking her head. "You know the choices." She started listing the acceptable activities—blocks, puzzles, markers and paper, playing a board game with a friend, or reading quietly by yourself—and warned, "If you can't decide, Monty, I can decide for you."

Monty didn't care what he did during recess—he just didn't want Mrs. Tuttle picking for him. Scanning the room, suddenly another idea burst into his head, just like yesterday. Sweet! The ideas were coming thick and fast as snow.

"Markers and paper!" he blurted. Because two kids were already at the markers and paper table: Jasmine and Lagu. And he needed to talk to them. Quickly Monty made his way over and sat down, and as quietly as he could, he explained his plan. He wanted Kieran, Winnie, and Finn to be his Buddies tomorrow. All three of them. He wanted them to stand with him while he told the parents about the books they had read, and he wanted them to sit with him and his parents during refreshments. And he needed Jasmine and Lagu to help get the message to them.

Jasmine was covering her paper with rows of pink hearts, yellow smiley-faces, and multicolored rainbows. "Why?" she asked.

"Because," said Monty, "it's snowing. So I can't tell them at recess, right? So I need you to tell Kieran at lunch, and Lagu, you can tell Winnie when you guys get home, okay?"

Lagu nodded, agreeing, but Jasmine made a scared face. "How come you can't tell Kieran? You sit with her at lunch, too."

"Because that's the only time I have to find Finn," argued Monty. "Come on, Jasmine. You know it's not fair."

Thinking, Jasmine added a row of daisy-shaped flowers. "Okay," she finally said. "I'll tell her."

Now Monty could hardly wait for lunch. When recess ended he filed down to the cafetorium with the hundred other kids who had second lunch. He put his lunch box on a tray and got a carton of milk and started wandering around, pretending to search for a seat. But really he was searching for Finn.

The problem was, he wasn't the only one wandering. Principal Edwards seemed to be doing one of her Every-Child-Known tours. She was walking up and down the rows of tables, greeting kids by name. Now her white head was swiveling toward him.

Monty froze. Maybe if he held perfectly still, she wouldn't see him.

She saw him.

"Montana!" she said, cheerfully. "How are you today?"

Monty tried to act normal. He hadn't done anything wrong, right? The principal was just saying hello. He managed to squeak out an answer. "Good."

"Let's see, I remember," said Principal Edwards. "You're at the nut-free table, aren't you?"

"Nut-free," he echoed, trying to agree with everything she said.

The principal started walking with him toward the nut-free table. What was he going to do? Outside, big flakes of snow were still hurrying down. Hurry! Think! Lagu was going to tell Winnie, and Jasmine was going to tell Kieran. But what about Finn? If Monty couldn't tell him, who could?

Sierra.

Sierra knew about the plan. Sierra was the kind of kid who could walk around the cafetorium without getting in trouble. Sierra could tell Finn.

"First I have to see my sister," he told Principal Edwards. "My twin sister," he added, because one of the good things about being a twin was that most people wanted to know what having a twin was really like. Mentioning that he was a twin might just distract the principal from the fact that he wasn't taking his seat at the nut-free table.

It worked! Principal Edwards started asking the usual questions—who's older? Do you ever have the same dream?—and Monty kept answering. Sierra was older. No, they didn't have the same dreams. But meanwhile, soft as snow, he glided over to Sierra's table. He took a plastic bag of carrot sticks from his lunch box and handed them to his sister, as if maybe they'd gotten into his lunch box by mistake.

And silently he mouthed the words, *Tell Finn*.

TOO LATE

Wednesday morning the kids on the bus were wild. Apparently the first snow had made some parents decide it was time for warmer clothes, and kids were tossing their mittens back and forth across the aisle.

"No throwing things!" shouted Mr. Milkovich.

The bus chugged down the last leg of the route, alongside the hill that tumbled down to the ocean. At the bottom of the hill the snow-dusted domes of the sewage-treatment plant looked like huge snowballs. The domes made Monty remember "Hidden Treasures from Your Toilet," which was still funny no matter what Mrs. Tuttle said.

But what was Mrs. Tuttle going to say today? Yesterday Jasmine, Lagu, and Sierra had gotten the message to Kieran, Winnie, and Finn to come find him at the Culminating Event, because he was going to be their Big Buddy. Officially. Which wasn't really true. He just wanted it to be true. But what if he got the kindergartners in trouble? That wasn't cool.

"So, my friend," said Mr. Milkovich as the bus pulled into the bus circle, "today you are quiet. You have troubles?"

Monty was sitting in his usual spot, right behind the driver. "Kind of," he said, staying in his seat as the other kids plodded up the aisle and stepped off the bus. "I think I'm going to be in trouble pretty soon."

"What kind of trouble?"

"The kind where people are mad at me," said Monty.

"So, it's no problem for you," said Mr. Milkovich. "You will—how do you say?—throw yourself on court."

"What?"

Mr. Milkovich took his big hands off the steering

wheel and tapped them to his big head, as if he was waking up his brain. "Yes, here we go! You will *throw yourself on mercy of court.*"

"What?" repeated Monty. "How?"

"If you are in trouble, confess. Beg for mercy."

"How do you know?"

"Can you believe me?" asked Mr. Milkovich. "Where I come from, I was judge. So, listen. It's good idea."

Monty stood and hefted his backpack onto his shoulder. "Mr. Milkovich, my friend," he said, "have a good day."

Up in Mrs. Tuttle's room the schedule for the day was written in blue marker on the whiteboard.

9:30   Mrs. Tuttle's fourth-grade students to cafetorium

9:45   Mrs. Calhoun's kindergartners to cafetorium

10:00	Families arrive
10:15	Musical entertainment by school band
10:30	Refreshments

At nine thirty, right on schedule, Mrs. Tuttle clapped her hands. "One two three, eyes on me! We will now line up to go downstairs. As we walk through the school, our noise level will be at *zero*. Our hands will be at our sides."

Monty and his class marched down the hall. Marched down the stairs. Marched through the front lobby, where Mrs. Tracy—*you can't cross over my bridge!*—waved at them through her big window. Then marched down the first floor hall. And then, finally, they were there. The cafetorium.

Overhead, a big banner said WELCOME! BIEN-VENUE! BIENVENIDOS! On one side of the room a long table held trays of muffins and scones and cookies, and pitchers of orange and apple juice. On the other side stood art easels holding student work. Buddies were supposed to meet at their easels. When the families arrived they would walk around, asking questions, and the students would answer.

Monty went and found the easel with his report on Leo, based on his five facts. And tacked up next to his report was a picture Leo had drawn to illustrate *The Tale of Samuel Whiskers*. Leo had colored the rat white with brown spots, just like Officer Samuel Scratcher McIntosh Whiskers the third. Monty wished Leo were here. He wished he could tell Leo how much he liked the drawing.

"We meet again," came a voice right behind him. "Good morning, Montana," said the principal.

Monty felt the too-late alarm go off inside him. He felt his heart thumping. Usually Monty got the alarm clock feeling when his dad got mad that he was taking too long to make up his mind. This time he'd made up his mind—but to do something he didn't have permission for, which was a sure way to make a lot of people mad. At him. And it was too late to change his mind back. *Help!* Monty hadn't figured this part out!

Desperate, Monty looked around for help. A few feet away stood Jasmine at her easel, her head speckled with pink barrettes in the shape of little hearts. Monty caught her attention and made a face: *Help!*

Through the yellow reading glasses perched on the tip of her nose, Principal Edwards studied the work on the easel. "Leo," she said, reading aloud the name in the corner of the drawing. "That's your Buddy?"

It was weird to think about how much grown-ups knew. They acted like they knew everything. But they didn't. They couldn't. The principal knew that his name was Monty. But apparently she didn't know that Leo, Monty's official Kindergarten Buddy, wasn't coming to the Culminating Event.

"It *was* Leo," said Monty. "But he moved away."

"That's too bad," said Principal Edwards, frowning. "Well, what now? Why don't you come along with me and look at the other student work."

"Um," said Monty, stalling. "I better stay here."

The principal's eyes seemed to get smaller as she trained her gaze on him. "If you don't have a Buddy to meet, why would you need to stay here?"

"'Cause I have some extra Buddies."

"Extra?"

Bit by bit, he explained. Some kids didn't get Reading Buddies, because they had special services, like speech therapy, and English as a second language, and—he didn't know all of the reasons. But he knew they wanted Buddies. So he'd been their Buddy during recess. Unofficially. But now that Leo was gone, he decided to be their Buddy. Officially.

Peering over the rims of her yellow glasses, Principal Edwards studied Monty. Probably she was thinking that her Every-Child-Known philosophy had been a mistake. There were some kids it was better not to know.

"Exactly who are these extra Buddies?" she asked.

"Sipping once!" said Kieran, running up and wrapping her arms around Monty's waist.

"Kieran," said Monty.

Winnie came up and got in the hug, too. "Sipping twice!"

"Winnie."

And Finn did a little dance while he said the last line, "Sipping chicken soup with rice!"

"And Finn."

"Kieran, Winnie, and Finn," repeated the principal, just as Tristan Thompson-Brown—the kid who teachers sent on errands, the kid who never got in trouble—came running over.

"Mr. Carlson needs Monty right away!"

Principal Edwards frowned. "Mr. Carlson needs Monty *now*?"

Tristan Thompson-Brown nodded his bright orange not-me head. And quickly, so Principal Edwards couldn't see, he flashed Monty a grin. Monty grinned back. Jasmine had asked Tristan for help! And Tristan had helped! Just then Mr. Carlson tapped his baton to his music stand, his signal for the band members to gather onstage.

"I better go," said Monty, giving the principal a what-can-I-do? shrug.

"Yes, you'd better," she said. But before Monty could take off she added, "We'll discuss this later."

Monty sprinted up onto the stage and squeezed into his seat between Ella and Emma. He got his flute from its case, stashed the case under his chair, and put the pieces together.

Looking as if his musical note bow tie was tied too tight, Mr. Carlson tapped his baton again.

"Welcome!" he cried. "We hope you enjoy our musical selections!"

When the band finished playing, the members who weren't in Mrs. Tuttle's class headed back to their rooms, and the Mrs. Tuttle kids went to sit down with their families and Kindergarten Buddies. Monty wound his way through the cafetorium until he found his group, sitting at the nut-free table. Except group wasn't the right word. It was more of a mob scene.

There were all three of his Kindergarten Buddies.

And there was Lagu with his Buddy. And Jasmine, who had to sit at the nut-free table, and her Buddy.

Then there were all the families, including Jasmine's mom, talking to Monty's mom, and Jasmine's dad, talking to Monty's dad. And there was his step-mom, talking excitedly to Mrs. Luka. It sounded like they knew each other from when the Lukas had first come to the United States. And there was his step-dad, holding Little A. And there was Sierra!

"How come you're here?" he asked.

"I got special permission," said Sierra, grinning, "since my whole family was coming."

"And I made a special snack for us that's nut-free," announced Monty's mom. She opened up a basket and started passing around blueberry muffins.

"Wait," said Monty, confused. "Why would you bring nut-free muffins?"

Monty's mom smiled a funny, crooked smile. "So we could sit at the nut-free table?"

"How did you know you wanted to sit here?" demanded Monty.

"I told her one of your Buddies was nut-free," explained Sierra, with an isn't-it-obvious? expression on her face. "Duh!"

"So I made nut-free muffins," said Monty's mom.

Monty stared at Sierra in horror. He knew she looked just like him: brown hair, blue eyes, freckles. And sometimes she knew *exactly* what he was thinking, which was cool. But sometimes she did exactly the *opposite* of what he would do.

"You *told?*" he said out loud.

"You didn't tell me it was a secret!" objected Sierra. "And I thought what you were doing was really great," she said. "Being a Buddy for three kids!"

"You did?" asked Monty.

Sierra nodded, and Jasmine joined her. They were like the Town Crier team. "Totally," said Sierra, and Jasmine agreed, "Totally."

"Besides, why shouldn't we know?" asked his dad, sitting across the table with a black box in his lap. "Look at this! Look what you've done!" He swung his hand around the table to include all the people sitting there. Monty and his three Buddies. Jasmine and Lagu and their Buddies. Sierra and Aisha. And all the grown-ups who went with all the kids.

"Look around you!" said Monty's dad. "It's awesome!"

Monty looked around at everybody eating blueberry muffins together, having a good time, and for about one second, Monty did see that it was awesome. And for that one second, he felt awesome! His dad was proud of him. He wished he could stay in this second forever. He wished he didn't have to confess that not everybody was going to think it was awesome.

"Thanks," he said. "I guess I was just worried because—um—I didn't really know if it was all going to work out."

"What do you mean?" asked his mom.

"Well, I told Mrs. Tuttle how I had three extra Buddies, and she said I could choose *one* of them, since Leo was gone. But I couldn't choose. So I didn't. So I never really got permission to be everybody's Buddy. Not officially."

Monty's dad touched both hands to his bald head, as if he was trying to keep it from flying away. "That's my Monty," he said. "The boy who couldn't make up his mind." But he was smiling when he said it, as if he wasn't mad.

"And mine!" said Monty's mom, smiling, too.

Beth waved a hand in the air. "I'm a fan."

And Bob, holding Aisha, said, "Me, too."

"He's my brother!" said Sierra. "My twin brother!"

Monty's dad wasn't mad. His mom wasn't mad. Monty felt like his single second of awesomeness was lasting more like a whole minute. And it felt good. Then he felt something else: eagle eyes. Trained on him. Across the cafetorium, the principal lifted her hand to point him out to the person she was speaking with.

Mrs. Tuttle.

ONE TWO THREE, EYES ON MONTY

Tiny Mrs. Tuttle charged toward the nut-free table, trailed by Principal Edwards. When she got there—which took about ten seconds—she spluttered, "Montana Greene! I honestly don't know what to say, Monty. This is so unexpected."

It was like she had said "one two three, eyes on Monty," and everybody had obeyed. Monty could *feel* everybody's eyes on him. He could feel the eyes of Mrs. Tuttle and Principal Edwards. Also the eyes of his mom and his dad. And his stepmom. And stepdad. And his sister Sierra and his friends, Jasmine and Lagu. Plus all their Buddies, and all the parents of all the Buddies.

The only person at the table who wasn't silently watching him was Little A, who crowed, "Buh! Buh!

Buh!" It was more a sound than a word, but Jasmine whispered, "She's saying Buddy!"

"Buh-*dee*," coached Sierra in a soft voice. "Buh-*dee*."

"Buh!" agreed Aisha.

After Little A had broken the silence, Kieran's mom spoke up. "Kieran just adores Monty," she said. "She said he reads them stories at recess because there isn't time during the school day. And I want to publicly thank Monty for going the extra mile."

Aisha crowed, "Buh!" again, and then another woman spoke.

"I'm Finn's grandmother," she said. "And I never saw Finn so excited about school as the day he came home and said Monty was his Big Buddy."

Lagu's parents were speaking to Lagu in Sudanese. Lagu listened, then said, "My parents say that Monty is helping Winnie learn to read. They say he's a special boy."

This was out of control. It was worse than Thanksgiving dinner, when everybody said what they were thankful for. Now everybody was saying nice things—about him! For a second Monty didn't know what to do, because he was starting to feel something he had never expected to feel, not in a million years—sorry for Mrs. Tuttle.

He felt sorry for Mrs. Tuttle because she was standing right where he usually stood: in the make-up-your-mind hot seat. Now Monty was the one with X-ray vision, able to see inside somebody else. He could see what his teacher was trying to decide. Should she stay mad at him? Or not? Monty knew how hard it was to get un-mad at somebody. But he knew what to do: throw himself on the mercy of the court, like Mr. Milkovich said. And for extra credit, Monty threw in Leo's puppy-dog eyes.

"I know you told me to make up my mind and pick one Buddy," he said, "but I *couldn't*. But none of the Buddies knew it wasn't okay with you. So if you have to take me, I get it,"—he held out his hands for imaginary handcuffs— "but let my Buddies go."

One two three, eyes on Mrs. Tuttle. Everybody

was watching her, waiting to see what she would say. Was she going to stay mad? Or show mercy?

"Buh!" crowed Aisha.

Tiny Mrs. Tuttle heaved a big, tired sigh. "I don't think we'll put you in jail, Monty," she said. "Not today, anyway."

Monty figured that even if his teacher wasn't acting mad, she wasn't exactly un-mad, either. This was more like a truce. But a truce with Mrs. Tuttle was a good deal for him. He'd take it.

"Thanks," he said. "Thanks a lot."

The principal put her hand on his shoulder and leaned down so her white hair and yellow glasses were right next to his face. "Mr. Greene," she said, "some of your decisions have been better than others, but you *are* making decisions. From now on, feel free to sit wherever you like at lunch. I don't think anybody could call you a waffler anymore."

Principal Edwards and Mrs. Tuttle moved on to make the rounds of the other tables. Monty took a swig of orange juice and another bite of blueberry muffin. Today was: the Culminating Event. The weather was: Snowy. And Monty was: Not a waffler.

Not a waffler!

Everything was just about perfect, except for one thing.

"I wish Leo were here," he said.

"So did he," said Monty's dad as he pushed the black box he'd been holding across the table. "He had an idea of something special he wanted to get you. He chipped in everything in his piggy bank, and your mom and I made up the rest, and, well—this is from all of us."

"Buh!" said Aisha.

"She's saying *box*!" said Jasmine.

Monty undid the clips. He lifted the lid. Inside a golden instrument was nestled in black velvet.

"A trumpet," announced Lagu.

"No way!" said Sierra.

"Way," contradicted Jasmine. "*Way* way!"

"Mom," said Monty. "*Dad*. Thanks!"

Now he could switch instruments, and nobody would accuse him of waffling. Monty wasn't sure whether his decision not to decide—his refusal to choose—made him more of an unwaffling waffler or a waffling unwaffler. But either way, he knew that *sometimes* he knew what he wanted. And when those *sometimes* came along, you had to stand up. Speak up.

There were good and bad things about being a twin. Getting lumped together in a parent's bad mood—not good. Getting dragged around to soccer tournaments to see your twin sister score goals—not good. But always having someone around—someone who knew exactly what you meant, someone who stuck up for you—good.

Maybe tomorrow he would go back to trying to avoid getting noticed. But today he was going to say what he wanted.

"Hey, Mom, Dad," he said one more time, "I don't want to flip-flop anymore. I want to go back to how things were before. Me and Sierra together."

"Me, neither," Sierra said. "I mean, me, too. I mean—I don't want to flip-flop anymore either. I want to go with Monty."

"That sounds good to me, too," said their mom. She reached across the table and took one of Monty's hands in hers, and Sierra's hand in the other. "You two belong together."

This time, Monty didn't mind being half of "you two."

Monty's dad agreed. "Sounds like a plan," he said, nodding, and he started talking to Monty's mom about which house Monty and Sierra should go to this afternoon.

"Dad, pronto!" said Monty. "While we're young, please?"

"Ouch!" said Sierra. "He got you, Dad!"

While his whole family was laughing, Monty felt a tug on his sleeve. It was Jasmine, crowned in pink heart barrettes.

"Are you never going to sit here at lunch anymore?" she asked. "Now that you don't have to?"

It looked like needing to make up your mind never stopped.

"No way," he said. "I'm not a jerk! I'll sit here sometimes."

Monty figured that sometimes he would sit with Jasmine here at the nut-free table. Because she didn't have a choice, and he did. And sometimes he would sit with Lagu at the regular fourth-grade table. He would even sit with Tristan, if Tristan stopped calling him Waffles. Which he should, because Monty wasn't a waffler anymore.

One of the best things about a Culminating Event was how long it took. By the time the families left, all Mrs. Tuttle's class had time to do was troop upstairs to get their coats and hats and mittens from their locker and head out for recess.

Outside, Monty headed for his favorite farthest-away place. The sky was blue and the playground was white—sort of. The snow that had fallen was mostly trampled, but on the other side of the fence, the jungly place where nobody went, the snow still lay clean and white. Monty yanked off his mitten so he could stick his hand through one of the diamond shapes made by the chain links. Scooped up a handful of clean, white snow. Nibbled it. It tasted like the sky, like if you could make a sky-flavored snow cone.

It had been a busy morning. Monty listed all the things that had happened so far.

Throw yourself on the mercy of the court and have the judge show mercy. Check.

Be declared not a waffler. Check.

Get a trumpet! Check.

Stop the flip-flop. Check.

Monty took another nibble, wondering if his rat would like snow. He added that to his list, one more thing to do: check out whether his pet liked snow. He could do that later today, after school. Right after he and Sierra got home.

ACKNOWLEDGMENTS

I am grateful for frontline readers Ann Harleman, Frances Lefkowitz, Ihila Lesnikova, and Elizabeth Searle; for Edite Kroll, my agent; and my editor, Lucia Monfried; and for the help and support of Gregory, Lydia-Rose, and Zora Kesich.

10